T0196483

SECOND
CHANCE

A story of one man's attempt to get into heaven after the
Second Coming of Jesus Christ, the World's Savior.

GARY VOCHATZER

WESTBOW
PRESS®
A DIVISION OF THOMAS NELSON
& ZONDERVAN

Copyright © 2017 Gary Vochatzer.

All rights reserved. No part of this book may be used or reproduced by
any means, graphic, electronic, or mechanical, including photocopying,
recording, taping or by any information storage retrieval system
without the written permission of the author except in the case of
brief quotations embodied in critical articles and reviews.

This is a work of fiction. All of the characters, names, incidents,
organizations, and dialogue in this novel are either the products
of the author's imagination or are used fictitiously.

Scripture quotations are taken from The Living Bible copyright
© 1971. Used by permission of Tyndale House Publishers,
Inc., Carol Stream, Illinois 60188. All rights reserved.

WestBow Press books may be ordered through booksellers or by contacting:

WestBow Press
A Division of Thomas Nelson & Zondervan
1663 Liberty Drive
Bloomington, IN 47403
www.westbowpress.com
1 (866) 928-1240

Because of the dynamic nature of the Internet, any web addresses or
links contained in this book may have changed since publication and
may no longer be valid. The views expressed in this work are solely those
of the author and do not necessarily reflect the views of the publisher,
and the publisher hereby disclaims any responsibility for them.

Any people depicted in stock imagery provided by Thinkstock are models,
and such images are being used for illustrative purposes only.
Certain stock imagery © Thinkstock.

ISBN: 978-1-5127-6572-4 (sc)
ISBN: 978-1-5127-6574-8 (hc)
ISBN: 978-1-5127-6573-1 (e)

Library of Congress Control Number: 2016919521

Print information available on the last page.

WestBow Press rev. date: 04/21/2017

THIS BOOK'S PURPOSE

In Noah's time folks were marrying, raising families, working, partying, and enjoying the fruits of their labor. Then God saw evil develop in their lives. Because of that "Sin has caused Him to grieve over His creation of humankind." He thus devised a plan that would put an end to this evil or so He thought!

Evil reared its ugly head again and thousands of years later, He once again was "grieved over the sin that developed in the human heart" and so He devised a plan, for the second time, to end this awful human behavior. Sadly, all of this sin was happening on the one planet He had set aside, out of the entire universe, to be the example for peace throughout His creation. This is the story of that second plan.

The Author
Gary Vochatzer

WWW.WHISPEREDTO.COM
CALENDARS / WALLET CARDS / BOOKS / POETRY

PRODUCT CREATOR: GARY VOCHATZER
6507 Pacific Avenue, #332 • Stockton, CA 95207
PH: (800) 698-9556 *FAX:* (209) 957-6014
E-mail: garyjv3940@yahoo.com

Over past 20 years, I have written:

- 500+ Poems
- 90+ Short Stories
- 50+ Biblical Statements
- 15+ Songs
- 5 Books published
- 5 Books ready to publish
- 25 Books written to be typed
- 225 Statements of Conscience

ALSO

- 27 years kept a daily diary
- 24 years kept a daily prayer journal
- 48 years a Christian
- Been a Life Insurance Broker for 52 years

CONTENTS

Chapter One

"THE VANISHINGS"

CHAPTER ONE
The Vanishing

It's 3 A.M. on a Wednesday night and I just woke up from a terrible nightmare but not remembering what the nightmare was couldn't be half as bad as the nightmare the human race is now living! So I got up from my bed without waking anyone in the house and went out to our dining room to sit and write out what has happened in the last <u>thirty-six months</u> in case no one else has, and for the benefit of those who will come after us, to let them know what we have been through and are, at this moment, going through. Worst of all, we are not seeing it get any better, so the future must be just as bleak!

First of all to those who read this material, let me first tell you a small bit of who I am so you won't think this is all a hoax. I am a middle-aged man who lives in a midsize town in this country, The United States of America. I have a college degree in computer programming and found a good paying job (six figures) at a nationally known computer company. I met my wife almost twenty years ago and we have two teenaged kids (boy and girl); we are (in my opinion) about as average as you can get. There isn't (I don't think anyway) anything unusual about us as a family or as individuals.

We start on Mondays by going to work. (My wife is a nurse at a local hospital.) Our kids both go to the same high school and a bus picks them up daily and drops them off two miles away from home each day. I work at a desk doing what's been put on my agenda in programming on a daily basis. We try to have dinner together, but a lot depends on (1) kids' activities and school homework, and (2) if the Mrs. gets an emergency call to come to the hospital to help. Seventy-five percent of the time we manage to sit down and eat dinner and discuss our day. On the weekends we mow our lawn, rake our leaves, take out the trash, watch TV, nap, go for a ride, go out to dinner, maybe catch church once in a great while or visit a relative. Again nothing out of the ordinary.

Well that about sums up who I am, who we are, and now I can feel comfortable about telling you what has happened to the "world" in the last <u>thirty-six months</u>. I know if you are an iota like me, <u>you are not going to believe any of this I am going to share and, to be honest, I don't know how to prove it unless you were here to witness it</u>. More than likely anyone who reads this is going to be a person who comes along long after the Mrs. and I are long gone. Enough said – Here is my story.

It was March and it was cold! It was the ninth day of the month and the world, our country, the United Nations, our town, our neighborhood, our block, my neighbor, our home, our jobs, our family were getting along as usual. There was nothing big going on worldwide that I can recall-no major wars, no shortages, and no governments were having difficulties. So in essence on March 9th, all was as it's always been-ordinary! That is until about 3 o'clock in the afternoon. I remember it as it if happened today! Here is what I saw, and it was sudden, in a moment, in a flash, at exactly 3 P.M. (I had just looked up at the clock in our hallway.) A number of people <u>vanished</u> from where they were standing, sitting, walking. All of a sudden they were gone, with absolutely no trace of them. They took nothing away with them but the clothes they were wearing. I looked around at 3:01 and was gasping, wondering what happened.

We have about five hundred employees at our company site. In my area of work there are about fifty of us within voice range. We all have cubbyholes or cubicles for office space, with carpeted panels that go from one cubicle to another and are only five feet high so it doesn't take much to stand up to see who's where. At 3:01 there had to be a least fifteen people gone!! They didn't all go to the bathroom or the break room. The workday wasn't over as yet. They just vanished into thin air! To this moment I can still see their faces, hear their laughter, see them come in, in the morning and leave at night. I knew exactly who left at 3 P.M. and who stayed. Naturally, I was one of them who stayed. Otherwise, you wouldn't be reading this report!

At 3:05 after the initial shock of seeing them all gone, the rest of us looked at each other over our cubicles and said, "Huh! What happened? Where is so and so? Where did they go without leaving their chair? Why did they go and the rest of us are here? What's going on that we don't know about?" It was crazy. Gals were crying, guys were screening, folks were running wild, and it was chaotic. Naturally the building was empty in about an hour. No message over the intercom. It was just the natural thing to do. Leave and head home!

I park in a six-story parking lot and I usually park on the third floor and as usual that's where my car was. It took until four-thirty to reach it. You couldn't understand a word anyone was saying. Folks were crying, screaming, running or had gone into a seemingly hypnotic state, so I just kept quiet. I figured there had to be a reason for all this. It hadn't affected me personally. I was still here. The company building didn't blow up. My car was still in its same parking space. So I said to myself, "There is an explanation and within hours it will be solved. No big deal"! Well, it took over an hour to get out of the parking garage and I was finally on the street in an attempt to get home, which is about five miles from work.

I thought it was strange seeing some cars in the middle of the streets, no one in them. Cars were still running with lights on and I saw several accidents. Apparently a person who vanished while driving ran right into another car, a utility pole, but fortunately I didn't see anyone laying on the pavement hit by a non-driver car! I have to say it was crazy driving home-cars with no drivers, busses without a bus driver, even saw an ambulance with no driver and yet it was inching along as if someone was at the wheel! I saw folks on their knees crying, some shouting, even saw a few folks with their fist clinched pointing it toward the sky. Traffic was absolutely the worst I had ever seen, horns honking, people putting their hands out their car window yelling all kinds of profanities and then there were those who helped folks who got hit by a non-driver car.

It's now five-thirty on March 9th and I am still only half way home as traffic is moving slower than a snail. I turned on my car radio to see if anyone knew what had happened and went from one channel to another. All said the same thing. "What happened in my office at 3 P.M. happened all over the globe at the exact same time and in the exact same way." No one escaped this event, whatever it was. There was no language barrier, no time barrier, no ethnic barrier, and no government barrier. It happened everywhere at the same time, but nobody knew why.

But who did this and why were only a few affected? I mean we had fifty folks in our work area and only fifteen vanished. Why not us, why them? What made us different from them or them from us? The radio had no answers and I was too confused and disillusioned and now getting too angry to turn on my auto laptop computer, which may have given me an answer or two. It was now almost seven P.M. when I finally arrived at home. The Mrs.'s car was in the driveway so that made me feel halfway decent. I could see the three of them in the house as they had all the lights on. I parked, grabbed my laptop, and hurried on in, only to find what I had just left!

My Mrs. was in hysterics, my two kids were crying. The television was blaring out on each channel what had happened at 3 P.M. today. It was as I had seen on the streets on the way home-chaotic! I put my computer away, tuned off the television, sat down at the kitchen table and asked them all to come and sit with me. Within a few minutes all four of us were sitting at our table with one conversation-What happened? Soon I said, "Let's calmly tell, one at a time, what happened at 3 P.M. today and just maybe we can make some sense out of what's going on."

All agreed and I said I would start, which I did and I told them all that you have read above. My Mrs. volunteered next. She was at the hospital at 3:00-doctors, nurses, patients, about twenty in the entire staff vanished but the most amazing part was there was not one newborn child left in the maternity ward, not one! (That was spooky!) She went through what I did in trying to get home as the hospital is about three miles from our home. There were car wrecks, folks crying on the streets, cars still running with no one in them; it was a mess, but she finally made it to the house.

Next to speak was our daughter. She told how she was in her last class of the day and school was about over. In fact the bell rang at 3 P.M., the same time this chaos started. But just as all the students stood up to go on out of our class, she realized that about five students had vanished! The other twenty including her just looked at each other along with the teacher. All were, as all of us are still, bewildered! She said she went out of the classroom and kids were yelling for their sisters, brothers, boyfriends, girlfriends, teachers, and friends who had vanished and they wanted an answer. Of course, crying and yelling was rampant as you can imagine with three thousand teenagers on one campus and all of a sudden ten percent are gone! The busses were stopped by too much traffic so both the kids walked home as we are less than two miles from the high school.

Our son spoke last and he said just about all the same thing as our daughter did. He was still in a stupor about this whole thing. He thought it's from outer space! At 9 P.M. like most Wednesday nights, we all had our homework done, a last snack for the evening, television is off and we are all hurrying to bed as our days start early. But tonight was different; no one wanted to go to bed for fear of what we might wake up to. It was discussed even at this late hour to call our closest relatives so I called my mom and pop and two brothers and a sister. All were frightened. All were as confused as we were, but none of our family had vanished. We didn't know if that was good or bad. Then we called the Mrs.'s mom and pop and her one sister and they were about the same as my family. None of ours were taken! It was 11 P.M. We all thought even though we had no way of knowing what tomorrow held, it was best to head to bed to rest up for tomorrow's events.

By midnight the sirens had stopped. The noise in the neighborhood had come to a halt except for the normal dog barking or cat meowing. Soon we all fell asleep with the chaos on our minds.

The alarm went off as usual at 6 A.M. I was the first one up, as usual, and being anxious headed out to get our daily paper. The headlines were the biggest I had ever seen "VANISHED." That was it. One big word that filled the entire front page. (I saved a copy. It's in the top right hand drawer of our bedroom dresser tucked under my socks.) I opened it up to read some articles and soon my Mrs. and two kids joined me to learn what had happened. Of course, we all looked at each other and said almost in unison, "We made it through the night." That brought a smile to all our faces. I tore the paper into sections and told all of them to read what it said. Then, in a somewhat orderly fashion, each told what it said.

My son was first. "Hey dad, says here planes crashed killing hundreds because the pilot vanished!"

My daughter said, "Dad, says here trains crashed all over the world because engineers vanished into thin air leaving trains going sixty plus mph. But thanks to computers, though, most of them stopped running when they vanished!"

And my Mrs. speaks up saying, "Hard to believe but it says here every maternity ward in all the world's hospitals had the infants vanish and those younger than seven years old who were in hospitals also vanished."

"I wonder why infants and those under seven," she asked.

I read and the one article that caught my eye was the one about churches and how folks were lining up in droves to enter, but the doors stayed locked as no one could be found indoors to unlock them. Seemed weird to me. It was 7 A.M. No one really knew if we should get ready for work and school, but after a vote we all decided that we would treat this situation as a rarity and do what we normally do. All got dressed, grabbed a bite of breakfast and by 8 A.M. walked out the door; there was no bus for the kids.

Cars were jamming our streets and we met chaos at 8:15 A.M. It wasn't that cold out so we asked the kids if they could walk to school amidst this traffic jam in our own neighborhood. They agreed. I asked the Mrs. if it worked best if we took one car-mine-and I would drop her off at the hospital and she agreed. Finally at 9 A.M. we got out of our driveway and inched our car to Main Street, which would take us to her work. It took until 10 A.M. to travel to the hospital. It was chaotic, but we expected this. We kissed, smiled, and soon she was headed to the back entrance to her work. I drove on to my job in a very slow manner as no one could pass anyone. I don't even think a cop car, fire truck, or ambulance could get through that mess but, eventually, at 11:30 A.M., four hours later, I got to my job. The parking garage was at best half full. My space was empty so I parked.

There wasn't, it seemed, a whole lot of activity going on for a company with five hundred employees. I went through security and made it without incident. Those I did pass went by me without speaking instead of the normal, "Good morning" or "How are you this A.M.?"

It was quiet, somber, and spooky! I got to my desk and the same thirty-five who didn't vanish yesterday were all here. (I was amazed as I thought I was the only true employee!) Our day's work is usually on our computer screens when we get to our desk, but this A.M. it was blank so naturally I asked out loud if everyone else's computer screen was blank and, as if almost in unison, all thirty-four said, "Yes."

Not knowing what to do next, we asked the person in charge of our area, "What do we do with nothing on our screen?"

She responded, "I don't know, but no one leave and I will go find out." She left and the office went into a buzz about yesterday's event. Soon our manager was back.

She said, "It seems the head honchos don't know what to make of yesterday as almost one hundred employees vanished into thin air and without those important, knowledgeable people it's going to take some time to figure out what they were doing so the rest of us can go back to work. So the company wants you to catch up on any work you have been working on, and if caught up, help someone who isn't caught up. Closing time, break time, lunch time will all stay as usual. Now let's go back to what we get paid for!"

With that all of us did exactly what was asked. The buzzing continued around the office up until the clock said 5 P.M. At that we all headed to our cars, still in fear of what had happened, with not a single answer to date. I got to my car and headed out. By now most cars and busses that had stalled or had their driver vanish had been towed away and off the streets so it was one hundred percent calmer than yesterday!

I turned on my radio and again it was channel after channel of predictions of what happened, yet no one really knew. I stopped by the hospital and it had also calmed down. My Mrs. saw me drive up so she came out and got in the car. We hurried home without any conversation. When we got to our house (traffic by now was bearable as most cars and accidents had been moved out of the traffic lanes), both of our kids were home watching television, trying to make sense out of what had happened.

My son said, "Well, Dad, Mom. The predictions are as follows: (1) Outer space folks snatched up those they had targeted to take with them to their planet; (2) All those that vanished had a rare blood and for reasons unknown they just vanished; (3) Those that vanished were aliens already and they just got called back to their planet; (4) The Bible's prediction of this event came true and all those that believed by faith got called up to be with God and those that didn't believe got left behind, so you/we have four choices to believe?"

"As for me, I don't believe any of the four. There has to be another one that makes common sense!" With that being said, we all agreed to turn off the television, get ready for dinner and crash. The Mrs. made an excellent meal. We all ate until there was no room left for ice cream and, as usual, we all ended up in the living room.

In fact, I said, "This is rare. All of us at home! Maybe this vanishing thing turned out to be a good thing for us as a family?" We all smiled at each other. We chit chatted about our day-who went missing and who didn't and all the variety of predictions we heard at work and at school. It got to be 9 P.M. on a Thursday night. So as usual, we headed to bed and by 10 P.M. it was lights out for another night's rest in our house.

6 A.M. Friday, it has now been two days now since the worldwide vanishing and still no one knows why, only a handful of suggestions. I got up first and on out to get the morning paper and to open it to read, "Jesus Christ Called the Faithful."

Huh? How could this prediction be when so many have been told? Well, it was a Friday. The weekend was upon us so I didn't give much thought to it and yelled out to all (as usual), "It's that time" and it was the Friday rush too, and lo and behold the school bus was running. Traffic had gotten back to halfway normal so the Mrs. said she could take herself to work and by 8:30 A.M. the house was empty once again and I was off to my parking stall.

As I was driving my five miles to work I always passed several churches including the one we attended on certain holidays like Easter and Christmas. This morning, however, I noticed on each church a big sign. Why, I have not the foggiest. It said, "Closed" in big letters and huge signs-Catholic, Mormon, Lutheran, Baptist, and Pentecostal! All of them had a sign that said "Closed." Most unusual!

I found my way to my stall, and on into the building where most folks this morning had a halfway smile, just as I did. I got to my desk, turned on my computer and nothing! Again I stood up and asked the other thirty-five of us, "Anyone's computer say anything besides nothing?"

All said the same "Zero." So again we asked our boss what to do and again she said she would walk the walk to hear the talk!

She did and thirty minutes later she came back through the door that she walked through at least fifty times a day. This time, however she had a look I hadn't seen before. She asked us to gather around and all of us knew something big was about to happen.

She spoke, "All of you know this is a major player computer company nationwide and worldwide. We provide business and government with computer knowledge and trade secrets with much sophistication. But without the input into this company of those one hundred people who vanished, the executives who run and own this company have decided to shut it down and lay off the remaining four hundred. All of us will get our severance checks, pension checks, overtime checks and any other monies due us. There is plenty of money to pay the company's debts. The executives apologize but see no other actions. Thank you all for being so loyal. You can spend the rest of the day cleaning out your office space. Thank you."

What!! This can't be I thought. I am only twenty years from retirement, fifteen even would be possible, but this, no way, can't be, there has to be another alternative. These guys have been in business forty plus years. Just because a hundred people vanish, they are giving up! Can't be, I must have heard wrong, but it hit me and it hit the thirty-four others whom I know as a family at work. What now? Where do I go? Who is going to hire me? If those guys who are major players in the computer field, world-wide, who's next? Who's available to go look for a job? How am I going to pay the mortgage, buy groceries? We can't live on the Mrs.'s check. She brings in less than one half what I earn.

I went to my desk space and just sat there starring at what I had been doing twenty plus years. It's all I know. It's the only real job I have ever had. I have had this same desk and chair ten years. What will I do with the rest of my life? I don't have any hobbies. I am not trained for anything but computer programming. My head was spinning, as this had to be one of those nightmares I can't wake up from, but slowly it sinks in. It's no dream. It's no nightmare. It's a reality. I am unemployed for the first time in my life and I am scared to death! But I did as the rest of the thirty-four did, found an empty cardboard box in the hallway and began emptying my drawers full of paper clips, pens, papers, and I took all of the pictures off my carpeted panels. I cleaned off the top of my desk leaving a computer to sit by itself.

At 4:30 P.M. I said good-bye to my boss. She even gave me a hug. I headed to my car with my filled cardboard box and my laptop, looked at my parking stall for the last time, passed and waved good-bye to security and got on the road that would take me home from this job for the last time. I drove by those same churches and even though the signs still said closed; folks were lined up two deep to get in. I couldn't figure that one out. I drove extra slow going home as I was extremely despondent, but if it happened to me at my company, it had to have happened to thousands, if not millions, of other folks worldwide. I got home. The Mrs.'s car was in the driveway. The kids were home as I could hear them talking in the house. I got my things out of the car and despondently walked in the house.

All three of them could see something was wrong and immediately said, "What's up?" "You have a cardboard box filled with what?"

So again I said, "Let's move to the kitchen table as it seems to be a good place to talk." We sat. I told them the whole story. They couldn't believe it. I was still in denial myself! No one had a word to say. All had had a tough day and even though it was a Friday, which was the night we got ready for the weekend and kind of celebrated, tonight there would be no celebrating. I was tired.

It was only 7 P.M., but I simply said, "I am going to bed. Thanks to all of you for understanding that which I can't understand. Goodnight!!"

I got in bed and pulled the covers over my head as I was hoping to shut out the world if just for one night? I went right to sleep and slept until 4 A.M. on a Saturday morning. I got up and quietly slipped out of our bedroom and headed out to the living room to turn on the television to see if anyone had come up with any more answers to the mysterious vanishings.

Chapter Two

"RECONSIDERING THE FACTS"

CHAPTER TWO

Reconsidering the Facts

Shockingly all the broadcast world was saying this same thing, "The Faithful had been called up as predicted in the Bible." Naturally I sat there stunned! How can billions of people get left behind if this is the truth? What kind of God would only call up a few and leave the rest of us to do what? Is there no more God? Has he left us out there to fend for ourselves? Why didn't someone tell me of this upcoming historical event? I don't remember any preacher on Sunday morning talking of this event. I was bewildered so I decided that if it's on every channel it must be on the Internet and I could get an actual copy of this mess! I got my laptop, set it on the kitchen table. All is quiet in the house, which is great at this moment. I got it turned on and went directly to my favorite news channel and had the information copied via the Internet to my computer printer. And sure enough what was being said must have come from these facts:

1) All newborn children worldwide <u>vanished</u>.
2) All children worldwide under age seven <u>vanished</u>.
3) <u>Graves</u> worldwide had holes in them where apparently those faithful got called up to heaven.
4) Only certain people <u>vanished</u> and after a thorough investigation of thousands and thousands of individuals it appears they were also faithful to God.

<u>No one else vanished!</u> And no one knows the exact count because it's such a worldwide happening! I sat there stunned at 5 A.M. on a Saturday morning. Our entire world had been turned upside down in less than a moment, a twinkle of an eye, zap, all those people are gone, <u>vanished</u>. It's so farfetched. I still can't believe it, even though I have a printout staring me in the face! I sat back in my kitchen chair thinking. How is it that none of the four of us vanish? How is it that

not one in my or the Mrs.'s family vanished? I couldn't think of any babies or anyone under seven in our family, but even so you mean to tell me not one of us, not one, was a believer? Again, I couldn't believe what was happening. I poured a large glass of O.J. and just sat. I thought what about all the other theories. The aliens, the blood type, and a host of others. Why have the world leaders come to only one conclusion? By now the sun had begun to rise in the east, and it looked like a nice day even though it was my first-ever workday unemployed! I just sat, staring. Why, why, why has this happened? Why now did God choose, if that's the answer? Why didn't our family vanish?

We went to church as much as most folks we know. Why didn't God wait until I was fully retired? Why didn't God tell us of his plan to do this vanishing act? What have we got to look forward to now? Is the world going to be different now? I remember the old fairy tale story of someone named Noah where God supposedly flooded the earth and killed all who were not in some big ship with Noah. Is this going to happen again if it was really true, which I doubt? My head was spinning with questions. I did not have an answer of any kind. It's almost 6 A.M. on a Saturday morning and I am dizzy from no answers!

I finally got up from my kitchen chair and walked slowly back to our bedroom, where my wonderful, loving, kind woman lay in our bed. We have slept together now for twenty plus years. I got back in bed and stared at the ceiling with my hands under my head trying to rid myself of questions that no one seems to know how to answer! I fell back to sleep until I heard the family rumbling around the house. It's 9 A.M.

"My son called out, "Dad is what I am reading from your computer printer true?"

I semi-yelled back, "Yep, so far." With that I got up (the Mrs. was in the kitchen making breakfast as I could smell the bacon!), went into the bathroom for a quick shower and I got dressed in my Saturday Project Clothes. It was nice enough outside to do some work. I went on out to meet the family. We all sat around the kitchen table while Mom, as we all like to call her, fixed breakfast.

Naturally by now all had read what came off the printer at 6 A.M. It sounded as if no one wanted to start a conversation so I simply said, "Any comments about the readout?"

My daughter asked, "Why weren't we vanished?"

My son said, "Dad, do you really believe this stuff?"

Mom said, "Let's eat!" It was a quiet breakfast. In fact, more quiet than I can ever recall!

Finally I said halfway through breakfast, "You know what we should do until Monday morning? Let's not discuss what happened because no one has any answers. So let's enjoy this weekend." In unison, all agreed.

Soon breakfast was over. All helped clean up, which was a standard practice in our home. I decided to clean up the yard so it was out to the garage, put rake in one hand and big garbage bags in the other. It was cool, in the mid-50s range, but not so cold you couldn't work in the yard.

I began raking when a neighbor came over and asked me-or should I say-made a statement, "Looks like you didn't vanish either, so what do you think?"

I said, "You know it's been rough since Wednesday at 3:00. The family and I have kind of agreed to set it aside until Monday. May I suggest you do the same?"

With that he turned and walked back to his house apparently unhappy I wouldn't discuss the issue with him. It took about three hours to rake all the leaves up to make the yard look halfway respectable. I put the four large bags of leaves out on the curb for Monday A.M. pick up and, after putting all the tools I had used away, I went into the house and collapsed on my favorite living room chair! By now it was way past noon and I told the Mrs. I was zonked with my manual chores and all I wanted to do was rest! She agreed and said she felt the same.

The rest of Saturday was about as normal as it could be with all that's going on worldwide. We all got to bed about 10:00 and fortunately I didn't wake up at 4 A.M.! Being so used to getting up at 6:00 without an alarm clock is going to be a tough habit to break. But for now, Sunday 6 A.M. I was awake, automatically, into the kitchen for a glass of O.J. I got Sunday's newspaper, read the headlines and news articles, which all agreed with what I saw and read yesterday. No other opinions are even being sought out. The World Governments, both free and totalitarian, all came to the same conclusion as no one had come forward to admit that they have some form of gizmo that makes people vanish! All were up by 8:00. I asked if anyone would like to go to church, even though it's not Easter or Christmas and all said, "Yes."

By 10:00 all had gotten dressed and we headed to the church we visited maybe two times a year. When we drove up, it had a big, massive sign on it that said, just as it had earlier in the week, "CLOSED!" What? How can a church be closed?

There were a whole lot of other folks at the same church asking the same question, "Why is the church closed?" Folks were knocking on the front, some peering through windows, some went around back to check. The minister's car was there. We had seen him driving around so we knew the car he drove. No lights were on and it just looked totally empty – weird!

There must have been a hundred people standing around and, of course, I heard the voices in the crowd asking, "Why didn't I vanish? I believed."

Or "I have been going to this church ten years, never missed a Sunday. Why didn't I vanish?"

Even heard one person say, "I sang in the choir, gave to this church, prayed here, and I wasn't called up. Something must be wrong."

After thirty minutes with the family sitting in the car and me standing in a crowd of not-knowing-what-to-do folks, I got back in the car and I told them all I would take them all out for an early lunch at our favorite restaurant. We found a table and I asked if our favorite gal waitress was working, "No." the new waitress said, "apparently she was one of those believers and she and her two kids vanished. So I took over her place. What can I get for you or do you need a few minutes to look over the menu, and don't forget we serve breakfast, lunch, and dinner twenty-four hours a day!"

She left. We all four stared at each other as if to say, "Huh!" It was like no big deal that those people just vanished. No one cares where to. No one suspects anything. I mean she had worked here at least five years and she vanished and the next hour/day they replaced her like you would a dead car battery! Something is wrong! We ordered lunch and ate with hardly a word being spoken; in fact, most folks in the restaurant were quiet, which I thought was a little unusual.

After lunch we got in the car and I got a great idea! So I said to the family, "One of the head honchos at work vanished. I surely didn't know he was a believer, but I do know where he lives, which isn't far from our house. Let's drive by and see what's going on, ok?" All agreed and we headed to his house, which, in fact, was only two blocks from our house. I parked the car, went up to the front door, rang the doorbell and, much to my surprise, his wife (I had met her before at company functions.) came to answer the door.

Startled, I said, "Hi, we stopped by because I know your husband, and my friend said he was one of those that vanished, and we were just driving in the neighborhood so we stopped by."

"Well," she said, "I would invite you in but my house is in disarray and I am about to have a nervous breakdown because I have been left alone and I thought I was a believer just as much as he was, and he left me in a financial situation I don't know how I am going to solve."

I asked her, "Well, didn't he have life insurance and what about his 401k and his Roth IRA and monies in the bank, and I also thought he was part owner of the company?"

Then in almost a flood of emotion she said, "The life insurance won't pay without a death certificate. His 401k is locked up because the company is folding. His IRA money is also locked up because it had something to do with the company. He did have some monies in our joint checking account but only enough to last me, at best, three months, and yes, he was a small percentage owner, but that's locked up also in the company's demise. And, as you know, I have never worked outside this house. So what am I to do in three months?"

I tried to settle her down and simply said, "Three months is a long time and I am sure by then all this will have worked itself out. Look, call me if you need a friend. My family is in the car so I have to get going, ok!" She shut the door with tears rolling down her face.

I walked back out to the car. Naturally they all asked, "What in the world happened?" I told them and that ended their conversation and questions.

I pulled into our driveway. We all went into the house. The sun was in its last stage of giving light to our part of the earth. No one was in any mood to talk. We turned on the television, but nobody really watched it as most of it was directed to all the vanishings worldwide. By 9:00 we were all in bed and all in unison said, "Good Night."

It was an ok night's rest, seemed like I tossed and turned more, but at 6:00 this inner alarm clock went off. Even though I didn't have a job to go to, I am wide awake after six plus hours of sleep. I go to the kitchen for my glass of O.J. Didn't want to start the day off negative so I didn't turn on the television, radio or laptop. I just sat and watched the sun rise ever so slowly in the east.

Soon I heard rumblings. The kids and mom were up and getting ready for a day's activities while I sat in my pajamas wondering what I was going to do today. All made their own breakfast. All said, "Hi, Dad" and by 8:00 A.M. all, including mom (who was off to the hospital) said, "Bye, Dad."

Amazing, it was just no big deal to see their father and husband sitting in his pajamas at 8:30, not dressed to go to work. He was not driving out the driveway waving goodbye. He was not sick to stay home. He was staying home because he was unemployed and unemployed because one hundred of the top thinkers in our company vanished with no trace of where they went. Somehow it just didn't seem right.

With nothing to do and nowhere to go I decided first to see how long we could manage without my six-figure income. I knew it would be tough, but I got out my laptop, pulled up my financial planning software, looked at our monthly bills, and looked at our cash assets. I summarized that we could possibly, at best, without losing our house or cars, last at least one year. That felt good and, for some reason, my anxiety dropped a couple of points! While I was working at my computer I got to asking myself if all that was happening was true.

So I went to the Internet and looked up the Bible and I went directly to the New Testament. At least, I know the difference between the Old and New. I asked myself why didn't that qualify me to be vanished? Anyway, I got to the New Testament, but that's where I had to stop. I didn't know where in this book was there talk of a vanishing or faith calling or whatever it's called. So I went to the dictionary part of the Bible and looked in the "V's" for vanishing, nothing! (Strange, I thought, that's what the news media and government called it.) Oh, how about missing? Nope. How about faith? Wow, all kinds of stuff but nothing about vanishing or missing in Faith. I was stumped! So I just started from A to Z. I figured if I did that surely I would find a word. Well it took me all the way until the "S" to find "Second Coming." I didn't know what that meant because I was unaware of the First Coming. I started searching this section and I found a lot about this event in the chapter called Matthew and it started in Section #24. I took some notes and here is kind of what it said:

In verse 4, guys were asking God when he would return and he said to them:

1) A bunch will show up claiming they are God. Don't get fooled by them.
2) Lots of wars are going to be going on.

3) Nations will rise against each other.

4) Famines and earthquakes will happen.

5) A lot of bad stuff is going to happen.

6) Lots of Christians will be tortured and hated because they believed.

7) Lots will give up their faith in fear for their life.

8) False prophets (whatever they are) will show up and lie like mad.

9) Sin will be rampant all over the world.

10) Love is going to fly the coup.

11) Whoever survives all the above will get saved.

12) Preachers, television, missionaries, the computer, movies, books, videos, so that no one can say they didn't know all the above was going to happen.

13) Whoever is going, best be ready and don't look back.

14) Hope you aren't pregnant.

15) Talks about babies. (They all vanished!)

16) Hope God doesn't do this in the winter. March 9th, that's spring, I think.

17) Also hope it's not on a Sunday. (It wasn't, it was on a Wednesday!)

18) Going to be a whole lot of persecution going on.

19) Says if God didn't plan on coming back we would land up killing one another.

20) Bunch of folks are going to say they saw God, but don't believe it.

21) Lots of folks doing miracles saying they are God; don't believe it.

22) It's possible for the Believers to even get deceived by these false rascals.

23) If folks say, "Come on out to see me do a bunch of miracles," don't go out.

24) God's appearance is going to be like lightning, fast and furious.

25) Soon as that happens, the sun's going to go dark (an eclipse?), the moon won't shine, the stars will stop shining, and powers that overlook the earth will shake.

26) God's going to sound his anger as a trumpet blast and the angels are going to gather those who kept the faith.

27) There isn't anyone who knows but God when all this is going to happen.

28) Before this event all is going to be great. Life will be one big party and folks won't believe any of the above.

29) Best be ready all the time because no one knows God's timetable.

Wow! Twenty-nine things I noted out of this one section. I sat back and just stared at my computer. Then I started asking myself questions. If all that had to happen before the vanishing then the opinion of all the governments is wrong because for all I know none of that stuff I just took notes on has happened. Now I was really confused! Then I asked myself, if all that had to have happened before I was born years ago or was it all supposed to happen while I am alive or is it all going to happen after the vanishing? Then I asked myself, "I wonder if God over the years switched things around and now it's the vanishing and everything I took a note on is still to happen?" Boy, was I confused. No wonder folks like me don't read the Bible, just too hard to understand!

By now it was 10 A.M. I was still in the kitchen, still in my pj's, still with the laptop staring at me with all those predictions out of the Bible. I shut it down, cleaned up the kitchen, went in and took a hot shower, got dressed in my Saturday Project Clothes and looked straight in the mirror and said, out loud, "Now what?" Do I go look in the classified for a job? Do I fix broken stuff around the house that needs fixing? Do I sit in front of my television or computer? Do I stay in bed? Do I go visit the kids at school? Do I go see how my loving Mrs. does her job at the hospital? Do I visit a neighbor I know kind of well? Do I go to my job I have had twenty plus years and see if anything is going on? Do I try to confirm all those Bible predictions to see if they are supposed to happen before or after the vanishing? I didn't know what to do because I was so geared to being at my desk at work at this time of day! I decided to just do nothing so I went to my favorite chair in our favorite room-living room, and I plopped down and gave a big sigh! And I just sat!

Chapter Three

"THE NEW RULERS"

CHAPTER THREE
The New Rulers

At 11:30 during the nap I was taking the phone rang and it was my Mrs., "Hon, have you heard the latest?"

"No," was my response.

"Well, a group of guys and gals at the United Nations have come on national television to claim they have been chosen by a supernatural power to rule the world. And so far no one has challenged them. Turn on the television. I have to go as the blue light for an accident case just came on. Bye."

With that I did turn on the TV and sure enough this group of ten folks were sitting at a massive table saying they are now going to be in charge of the world and that they have been commissioned by a higher authority than humanity! Wow!! This immediately threw me to that section of the Bible I just read where it said, "A bunch will show up claiming they are God. Don't be fooled by them!!"

This was spooky, spooky, spooky! I got back on the Internet and sure enough it was all over the place about this statement by those United Nations people. I called my Mrs. back but she couldn't come to the phone. Kids are in class so can't call them. I know, I will hike down two doors to an old buddy neighbor who has Mondays off and chat with him about this stupid statement.

Out the door, a short brisk walk, a knock on the door, and he answers, "Hi, neighbor. What have you been up to?"

"Nothing much but don't have time to talk as we had a bunch of kinfolk who vanished and we are trying to help out those who got left behind so maybe some other time." With that he closed his front door.

I walked slowly back to my house. It was a cold day, overcast and a prediction of rain. It's 3 P.M., kids will be home soon so kept house nice and warm for all.

Sure enough they walked in shivering at 4:30, their normal time and half hour later the Mrs. drove into the garage and parked her car and came in. We gave a peck to one another. She got warmed up and asked if anyone was hungry. We all said yes so she began preparing a meal. The kids were in their rooms doing homework. I went out to the kitchen and sat at the table.

Soon I asked, "What are your thoughts on that announcement on TV you called me about?"

"Well after thinking it over and thinking about the vanishing and talking with a couple of other nurses we kind of thought maybe it's not such a bad idea having a one world government. After all it will save us time and money from all those stupid elections we go through every four years and think of all the money we will save by not having to have to pay all those politicians for doing nothing! Anyway, I guess if I had to make an opinion, I would say go ahead. Just be wise in your decisions."

I gasped in disbelief and said, "Honey, I read the predictions in this vanishing thing and those guys and gals are doing exactly what the Bible predicted. We can't be fooled by them!"

She stopped what she was doing and looked me straight in the eye, "I have been married to you enough years to know you wouldn't know the Old Testament from the New Testament so what gives with you and predictions?"

I said, "I got on the computer and tried to find some answers about those vanishings and I found in the New Testament all about this situation in a chapter called Matthew and it's in Section Twenty-four. I counted 29 predictions. This statement on TV was the first one of the 29."

With that she said, "Call the kids please. Dinner is about ready."

I went up to the kids' rooms and told them about dinner and they both asked me, "Dad, what is going on? Over 300 kids are missing from school and no one knows where they went. They are just gone. That's 10% of our entire school population. Have you got any answers?"

I said, "Yes, but let's not talk about it now. Let's go and have dinner and maybe later on tonight I can share some insight with you both."

All of us sat down to dinner and hardly a word was said, except for, "How's school or how's work at the hospital or how was your first day at home alone?" None of those questions got more than an "OK" answer.

We all cleaned up after dinner. The kids went up to finish their homework. I went to sit in my favorite chair and soon the Mrs. just about fell on the couch exhausted from a day's work and dinner. After a while I asked, "Do you want to talk about what was discussed in the kitchen?"

She said, "No, you have an opinion. I have an opinion. We are married, but we are still two different individuals, right?"

I said, "Yes!"

With that she said, "I am zonked and so I am heading to bed early. OK with you?"

I said, "Sure, Love." She did exactly that and I sat.

I knew the kids turned their lights out about 9:00 so I went and knocked on each door and asked if the three of us could talk so I could share my notes off the Internet this A.M. They agreed. I told them what I found out and when I was through they looked at me like I looked at the computer this A.M. – Dumb-founded! It was late. They didn't have any questions. They simply said they were tired and they needed their rest. With that I headed to bed exhausted and confused. I slept all night.

It's Tuesday and my second day unemployed. 6 A.M. up to do what I usually do. The Mrs. and the kids did what they usually do and by 9 A.M. I was alone again trying to work out what I want to do for the next eight hours. I know I didn't want to fix a bunch of stuff around the house. I have to really be in a fix-it mood, which I wasn't. I didn't want to watch TV, or look at my computer. I wasn't one to do a lot of just talking.

I don't have many hobbies, but I do play racquetball with a couple of guys I haven't seen in a while. So kind of got excited about that and into a shower I went, put on shorts, tennis shoes, T-shirt and a jacket and grabbed my racquetball bag, got in my car and headed to the club I belong to, which is only a couple of miles away. It is amazing that everything seems to be so normal for what just happened less than a week ago-traffic, people on busses, kids playing (must be over 7 years old?), and chimney smoke. The only thing I did notice was no moms pushing babies in strollers (guess they were right when they said all babies worldwide vanished).

It took me about fifteen minutes to get to the club. I parked (not many cars in the parking lot), got out, grabbed my gear and headed into the club. This is a plush club-the newest and best of everything and always spotless and it looked almost empty. I was used to a place packed with people. Maybe a workday and no one here? I walked up to the front desk, pulled out my card and handed it to the gal. She checked me in on their computer and said, "Have a good workout."

I said, "Thanks, but where is everybody? This place usually swarms with people."

She said, "Well, since you asked, here is what happened. The owner and his wife and two small children vanished last Wednesday at 3 P.M. We have not seen any of them since - no note, no phone message, nothing on his computer, no e-mail, no fax, zippo, just gone, and he leaves us to run his business. He also left a million dollar home with tons of furniture. They had a swimming pool and all sorts of other amenities. Now it just sits empty. Our second-in-command guy has kind of taken over but with no real authority. I guess a lot of the club members are aware of it and it's kind of spooked them from coming in. It's been real quiet and that's the story so far!"

With that and the fact that no one was here to play racquetball I kind of did what the others had done. I got my card back and turned around and headed to my car, backed out and drove off back to the house. I saw our favorite neighborhood shopping center so I pulled in to go in the grocery store to pick up a few items I noticed we were getting low on at the house, and found a parking place and went in with my racquetball clothes on.

Folks kind of looked at me as most were wearing heavy clothing, since it was only 45° outside. I tried not to pay no attention to their thoughts; grabbed a basket and began my stroll up and down each aisle looking to see what I came in to buy without a list (which is what I usually have) and again, all seemed so normal for what just happened. I was amazed at how quiet everyone was, almost suspicious looking at one another. I got what I came in for. I went to the quick check out, had it bagged, paid for it, and noticed one of the checkers was missing. I always saw this particular checker when I came into the store. So I asked the young lady who waited on me how the person was. Her response was, "Vanished last week." "Next please."

Wow! I walked past the tabloids and glanced at their front covers. "Aliens snap up Humans." "God has called those who believed, the rest of us will parish, just as in Noah's day." Naturally I didn't buy any of them because they are known to print the "gossip"! Out to my car, bag in back, head home to try to figure out what to do with the rest of a Tuesday. Got home, got the mail and in it was a letter from my company. Into the house with the groceries and mail, I sat down to open this envelope and began to read it.

"Dear_____(me), as you know the company was forced to close down due to the vanishing of our top brains and employers of this fine company. Those left to make a decision thought it was best to do as they did. We are terribly sorry for such a short, dramatic notice. Enclosed is your severance pay check, your unused sick leave paycheck, your one month's salary as a gift from us as a gift to you knowing well what you are going through, and also your 401K monies. You need to roll that into an IRA if you don't want to be taxed on this check. We already held out all the deductions from all the other monies, except for the 401K. Please accept our apologies and the best to you and your family for your future."

I again sat. I really thought all this was just a bad dream and I would wake up to find none of this true, but this letter confirms it. I am out of a job and at this age don't know if I can find one and am not capable of nor interested in starting my own company. I sat there for thirty minutes, looking at those checks and this letter. I was again – Dumb-founded!

I got up from the kitchen table and went over to turn on the faucet and slowly with my hands cupped put cold water on my face. It felt good! I looked at the rest of the mail and it was a couple of usual bills and junk mail so I went into the living room, almost fell into my chair, grabbed the channel surfer and turned on the TV. I sat up in my chair as I thought I was watching a cops and robbers movie, but this was a news channel!!

I was seeing and hearing police chasing men and women out of peoples' homes and businesses where the people had vanished or left them empty. Wow! From a helicopter camera, you could see people running out of the vanished ones' homes, carrying all kinds of stuff. Let's see. There is a guy with a TV in his arms. Wow! A gal was running with a whole bunch of clothes still on hangers. Wow! This is wild. This is stupid. This is dumb. How do they know those folks vanished? This is terrible, reminds me of when that incident happened in Watts, California, way back when I was a kid and saw all those folks breaking business windows; that was a rampage. I hope the cops capture these thieves.

Then I thought "I wonder if any folks on this block vanished. I know our neighbor to my east and west didn't and I have seen our neighbor across the street leave for work. But I just don't know." I kept watching what seemed like a movie instead of real life, but this was really happening and the station took me over to a few other countries and apparently this idea of looting vacant houses and businesses has caught on worldwide. It's scary! About fifteen minutes of that stuff was about all I could handle so off went the TV! And on came a nap!

I haven't done this for so long. In fact, I can't recall the last time I took a nap on a workday afternoon. But it felt sooo gooood! Slept until around 4. Decided to get out of these racquetball clothing and put on my Saturday Project Stuff. Before I knew it the clock said 5. Kids are walking into the house and the Mrs. just drove up. It's good to see the family as I can attest to the fact that it does get lonely in a house with just me here!

All said 'hi' and all looked exhausted so I casually asked the kids how their day was. "Not so good," both said.

"Why not," I asked. "Well that vanishing thing has left a lot of folks who run this school in real turmoil.

Listen to this, my son said, "Teachers have vanished, about twenty I heard. Kids' parents have vanished, leaving kids on their own and they haven't the slightest notion what to do. After all, they are like us, just kids! And of course they can't understand why their mom and dad or mom only or dad only got taken without them. It just seems weird. And with twenty teachers vanishing it left a whole bunch of kids without a class to go. The principal stuck them all in other classes which now makes our class size a whole lot bigger than it was before this vanishing thing happened!"

My daughter didn't say a word. Apparently her brother about said it all. My only reaction was, "Wow!"

Soon the Mrs. called out that dinner was on the table. We all sat down and began to eat. The Mrs. asked me how it was going with not going to a job now for two days. I kind of grunted as I really didn't want to go into what happened at the racquetball club or the grocery store or even the checks that came in today and certainly not the looting I saw on TV. But I did say, "I took a nap today for over an hour, something I hadn't done in years! If folks ask, there was no 'feeling guilty' about it."

That got a chuckle out of all of us! Soon we cleaned up our dishes, made sure we all did our part in the kitchen since mom does her part in cooking for all of us every night. We kind of all sauntered into the living room. It was only six thirty and I shouldn't have, but stupidly did turn on the TV and there it was-the same thing I had watched this afternoon.

All eyes in the living room were watching and of course, almost in unison, all three said, "Is this for real? What we are seeing?"

I softly said, "Yes."

"What's happening today? Why are all those people robbing other peoples' homes and businesses? What right do they have to do such a horrible thing? Why aren't the police stopping them? Where are the people who live in these homes? What's going on Daddy?" my daughter asked.

All I said was, "Honey, the world changed last week and this sort of thing, I guess, was expected to happen. After all no one is living in those houses and no one is running those businesses. Folks hear about it, see it vacant, and I guess just decide to take advantage of an unlawful opportunity!"

Apparently that stopped the questioning. We channel surfed thinking something decent, like a movie or a sitcom would be on. But apparently the TV industry thinks the world needs to know what's going on worldwide since this vanishing thing happened at the exact same moment worldwide. I guess if we wanted to watch a movie we could pick one out of our video library but no one was in the mood for that after watching the horror going on worldwide. I have to admit it was gruesome seeing the looting, fighting and, in some instances, we even viewed guys and gals getting shot and killed for what they were doing! Right on TV!

By 7:30 we all had had enough for the night and day so we all said we were bushed and tired. Each slowly headed to bed. The kids had no homework. I guess that was because of all the confusion at school. Tomorrow would be one week since the vanishing and I heard in some TV reports that lots of folks are scared to death that it may happen again at 3 P.M. Personally, I don't think so! By 9:30 the Mrs. was in bed, the kids' lights were on as I could see underneath their doors and I, being zonked from another bummer day, decided to call it a day and lights out—couldn't sleep! (Probably because of that nap!)

I reached across our bed and tapped my Mrs. on the shoulder and said, "Honey, are you awake or asleep?"

Surprisingly she said, "Yes, I am awake and to be honest I haven't slept a wink since you turned the light out at 10."

So I asked her, "Babe, is there anything I can do to help you in your day? Run an errand, take you guys out to dinner instead of your cooking, clean the house, fix anything you want fixed, anything?"

She said, "No Honey, there isn't a thing. You just work on doing what you need to do to find out what you want to do for the rest of your working years. What would make me content is seeing you contented."

Then I said, "That is really sweet of you. Tell me how things are at the hospital. If you don't want to, that's really alright. I know you need your rest."

She said, "Well, I can't sleep so maybe if I share with you what's going on it will get it off my chest and then maybe I can go to sleep. Anyway it's a mess! About ten doctors and the same number of nurses vanished last week. That naturally left the entire staff of a little over a hundred of us to do all the work without those very, very important people. The strange part is we didn't know they were any different than us! They were nice people, never saw them out of order, never heard any gossip about their character. Other than that we can't figure out what they had that we don't have. Car accidents from last Wednesday's vanishing have crammed the hospital. Sad, but I guess fortunate, the children's wing is totally empty because all those kids under seven vanished.

We have turned that wing into a virtual emergency space. Then our maternity room, as you know, also got emptied but we have a large number of pregnant gals who are giving birth or expecting and that room, in just this short time, is already filling up. Anyway it's the worse chaos I have seen in all my years of nursing. I have to say that out of all those situations I just talked about, the one that seems to bother all of us, is why those twenty, and not us? Are they the fortunate or are we the fortunate. It's just strange."

Then I said, "Wow, that is really spooky. Would you like to hear a moment about something that affects the two of us and I won't go into all the other stuff that went on in my life today."

She said, "Naturally."

"Well today I got the checks in from the company. It is a fair amount of monies we can put into the bank but not near enough to pay off all our debts and put the kids through four years of college. I am going to have to find a job but feel so fortunate that we are financially stable and I hope that makes you rest at ease, at least money-wise."

She said, "Yes, it does and I really thank you for sharing that! But another quick question is that I still don't understand why, just like the twenty doctors and nurses, how in the world did one hundred of the top people in your company vanish? That's twenty percent of the entire company that's gone! And I ask, were you so different from them?"

With that I said, "Sweetie, you and I will never, in a thousand years, know the answer to why some vanished and some didn't. At least so far, no one knows. Anyway, I'm tired as I know you are too, so go to sleep and I will see you early morning!"

Chapter Four

"REALITY SETS IN"

CHAPTER FOUR
Reality Sets In

6 A.M., I was awakened with one thought on my mind-to answer the question of why some people vanished and why others like us didn't. There had to be an answer! Out to the kitchen for my usual O.J., and, as usual I heard the three of them start rumbling, showers, music, doors opening and closing, and by 8:30 all were in the kitchen fixing a quick bite, then out the door as I waved good-bye to them. Still in my pj's I sat at the kitchen table and got out my laptop, turned it on and went directly to a favorite chat room where I talk every once in a while. I typed in, "Question – Who knows why some folks vanished and others didn't? Need ASAP."

I fixed myself a piece of toast and waited. Soon my computer lit up like a Christmas tree and the biggest portion of answers were, "It's in the Bible, Dummy! This incident has been predicted two thousand plus years. Those that believed in Jesus Christ (who died for our sins) and lived out their life as a believer, plus all babies and those under seven who knew not what sin was, have been called up, no matter who they were-rich, poor, male, female, doctor, horse manure sweeper. God knows the heart of all those who vanished to His heavenly home. Now we are left to deal with what's on the horizon and it is not looking good. That's your answer. Start reading your Bible!"

Huh! What! Then the TV statements were all true. No aliens, no blood disorder, no foreign interference, it was God who did all this to His creation! Man, I was mad! Why didn't someone tell us? Why weren't those ads on TV about this event? Why didn't preachers tell us, even if I only went to church two times a year? They should have said something! I was ticked, frustrated and I stayed so angry. I walked through the house. I started to cuss, but I held back. I looked out the window at all those other folks who didn't apparently hear it either, otherwise they would be gone, but they're not. They, like me, are still home. "How could this happen? I kept saying over and over. Why didn't we know? Who is responsible for most of the world not getting vanished!!

After an hour of ranting and raving within, I gave in and took a shower. For me that always helps when these kinds of things happen. Maybe I should have thanked God for all I have rather than ranting and raving, followed by only a shower. I got dressed in my project-to-do clothes. It was 11 A.M. and I was just so frustrated I didn't know what I was going to do with the rest of this day. I was hungry and I felt like I had to get out of the house so I went to a noisy coffee shop to get lunch. Parked my car and went in. A few folks were eating or reading the paper. I sat down at the main counter to eat.

The waitress waited on me and said, "Hi, whatcha going to have?"

I said, "Oh, how about a cheese burger, fries and a Pepsi?"

"Okie, dokie," said the young waitress. No one else was sitting at the restaurant counter area so I just kind of looked around doing what most call 'people watching.' Took about ten minutes, but soon my food and drink are in front of me.

The waitress then said, "Enjoy, this could be your last meal!"

I said, "What? What does that mean?"

She said, "You mean you haven't heard?"

I said, "Heard what?"

She said, "It was a week ago today at 3 P.M. when millions and millions of folks all over the earth vanished and some folks believe it's going to happen again at 3 P.M. today, so what do you think, is this your last meal?"

I said, "Nonsense, don't you read the Bible? It was a one-time vanishing and it's done. It's not going to happen again!"

She said, "Well, everyone has an opinion. Enjoy."

I told her to wrap up my lunch and I would go home to eat it. She said that she felt sad if she said anything to upset me as she was under the opinion everyone knew!

I guess that's what I get for not watching that stupid TV! I am still angry from this morning and I can feel it, almost feel like taking an alcohol drink, but I know by my family history that's a dead end street! Out to my car and head home, park, and in to sit alone at my kitchen table and eat a now-cold burger and fries and help it down with a soda. I had to get a grip on my mindset.

I simply had to get beyond this anger mood, so after eating, I went out to the living room and sat on the couch and spotted this huge family Bible sitting on the coffee table. It was a gift from someone and it's never been opened! So not knowing where to go first I simply started at Genesis, First Chapter. I read and read and read! None of it did I understand, not any of it. It all seemed so preposterous as I was raised to believe in the Big Bang Theory and that didn't include God!

So here I am, confused again! Do I believe, all those teachers, books, professors, classes, lectures on what they thought was right or do I believe what I am reading at this age in my life? I have taught my kids and allowed them to be taught the Big Bang. My Mrs. believes that theory, as do my mom, pop, siblings, her mom, pop, sister. All believed the same, so now what am I supposed to do, tell everyone I changed my mind, at my age?

Anyway, I set the book down off my lap after reading five chapters. I was confused! It's going on 3 P.M. and I started thinking of that waitress's comments. Could she be right? Will there be another vanishing? My heart started pumping and my hands got sweaty. I wonder who else thinks this nonsense. I grabbed the channel surfer and switched on the TV. Sure enough she was right! It is hysteria all over the world. I had no idea of this thinking! With an hour to go, the whole world is in a panic and I'm sitting here reading the Bible! I have to be crazy, but on the other hand what else should I be doing?

I decided to call the hospital to see if I could catch my Mrs. to tell her this "nonsense" but she was in the emergency room and was simply unavailable! I thought I would drive over to the school to see if I could find the kids in order to tell them. I went out to the car, drove down the street and there was traffic galore! Only a little time to go and I am trying desperately to get to my kids' school to tell them that they or me or their mom or whoever or no one may vanish very soon. Hallelujah, I am going crazy!

I got to the school at 2:50, raced to where I knew their last classes were and by 2:58 I had both of them in my vision. I caught up with them and at 3 P.M. they were both next to me. I looked at my watch and it was 3:01. Nothing happened and they, of course, said, "Dad, what are you doing at school?"

I didn't say anything but gave a sigh of total relief. I wasn't about to expose them to the whole story so I simply said, "I had nothing to do so I thought I would come over and give you two a ride home!" They both laughed at such a silly thing which was okay with me!

We made it home. They were both thankful and said I should do this more often. It breaks the bus monotony. I said fine. It was 4 P.M. They kind of crashed, but they unfortunately turned on the TV and as sharp as my kids are, they soon figured out why I picked them up. They both came into the kitchen and simply gave me a hug, no words, just a hug. It was now 5:00. The Mrs. drove into the garage as usual, into the house, into the kitchen, and within thirty minutes we were all seated to have dinner. My wife seemed extra tired so I asked if all went well at the hospital today.

She said softly, "No," then began to cry!

The three of us looked at her and we began to cry as none of us knew what was going on with the world! Soon I got back my composure. My wife had left the table and had gone to our bedroom.

It seemed that even though she cooked a fabulous meal, no one was hungry! I got up and asked the kids to clean up. I went back to console Mom. I went into our room and she was sitting on the side of the bed. I sat and put my arms around her. She wept openly for the first time I can ever recall. It got to me! It took thirty minutes and a cold towel to get her to just stop crying.

There was no need to talk. She, as well as all of us, just needed rest. Without her getting undressed I laid her down on the bed. After I unfolded the covers, I put the covers back on her and in a moment she was asleep, lights out and I slipped out to see how the kids were doing. They both didn't want to talk so I simply said goodnight and closed their doors. I then went back to the living room and again set this large book called the Bible on my lap. I opened it again, trying to see if I could glean just a bit of information in order to help me understand why all this is happening. By midnight I was exhausted, my eyes were hurting, and I felt like I was getting nowhere in my comprehending this book that I have neglected ever since I could read, at age 7! Why can't I seem to believe what it says? Why can't I seem to grasp its meaning? What's holding me back from having an ounce of faith in what I am reading, that it could be true?

Tired, I set the book down and headed to bed where I simply fell on it, pulled a cover over me and was asleep in a moment's notice! For the first time in years the entire family awoke, got dressed, left for work and school and I slept through the entire process. Guess I am more tired that I realized! It's almost 10 A.M., which means I slept ten hours. Wow! Still I am shook up over my inability to comprehend that Bible. Here I am a computer programmer and can't understand, or should I say, believe what I am reading. Anyway, fully clothed at 10 A.M. later than my usual practice, so undressed and into a shower, dress in other clothes, out for my O.J. and now sit at my kitchen table asking, "What's next?"

I decided instead of viewing the TV, I would go to my laptop and ask my favorite chat room what's the latest on planet earth. That brought in a flood of comments. I looked them all over and found most of them unbelievable. The one that caught my eye was this new world government. It seems that in just a week's time the USA, Russia, China, Cuba, Mexico, Canada, all the European countries, the Arabic countries, again, all agreed to a world government run out of the United Nations Building in New York. They plan on some way of having a new monetary system and a food distribution system Why, I don't know. I have heard of nothing regarding food problems. The last thing they want to run is the gas and oil industry, but Shell and Chevron won't go for that. Anyway, it's spooky, and it's just so hard to believe all this has happened in such a short time.

It's a Thursday. I decide to look in the classifieds for computer programmer positions. Of course, I ask, can one pay me what I was receiving? Am I too overqualified to find a halfway decent job? What's out there for me to even consider? I search until one pops out that looks somewhat attractive. I got my computer up and going and find this company on the Internet, check their website and ask for a printout of an employment application. Immediately, it comes. It took me an hour to fill it out. I faxed it to the department that does the hiring and now I just wait.

But I am not going to sit around doing nothing. It's noontime. I think I am going to take a walk down my neighborhood street and see if any homes are empty because folks vanished. So out the door and headed west. Nothing seems out of the norm. Yards are clean. Leaves have finally all fallen and have been hauled away! Things are beginning to start to bloom again. It's about 55°. By the time I get to the fifth house all seemed about as calm as a placid lake but then the tenth house looked out of place-yard unkempt, two cars in driveway, no smoke coming out of chimney. Most folks always have a fire going, if home. Lights are on, even the porch light, and it just seems odd as we live in such a neighborhood where folks really take pride in their yard and home.

I asked myself, Vanished? Back in the back of the house and just not visible? Friends picked them up and took them somewhere? Out for a walk like me? What will I say if they answer the door at my knock, "Hi, I live ten houses down and I just thought I would stop by to say hi!"

Anyway I stood there and finally got up the nerve to go to the door and knock. I rang the bell, again knocked, no answer, walked around back and knocked on back door, no answer, back to the front door, again knocked and rang doorbell. Nothing. So I gently tried the front door and to my surprise the door opened. My heart and feet were pounding with nervous energy.

I yelled out, "Anyone home?"

No answer back, so I slowly walked in. You could tell no one had been in the house for a while. It was cold, damp, but lights were on throughout the house. I walked through each room, one at a time; living room, dining room, kitchen, hallway, back bedroom, both bathrooms, closets, and still no sign of anyone. I went out the back door to check the garage. There was no one. So, back in the house I started looking at things and I turned off the lights as I left each room. I just had to believe these folks vanished. I had been in the house twenty minutes and decided to go when I saw a Bible sitting on the kitchen table so I kind of went over to it and slowly opened it. It was worn, all marked up with lines under certain sentences. It had been read, used a whole bunch, just by the look of it. Then I knew for sure that whoever these two were had vanished.

I started out the door and noticed a bunch of pictures on the fireplace mantle so I went and looked through them. It was funny that I had never noticed this couple, probably in their sixties based on the pictures, in our neighborhood. Sadly, we all live so close to one another and yet so far apart inside our house! I turned all the lights out (wasn't sure it was the right thing to do), went out to their mailbox and brought all the mail in and put it on the kitchen table and left.

I walked back to my house totally bewildered. I just couldn't come to grips with how one house and two people vanished and all those in between were left behind to deal with whatever it is we are going to have to deal with. It was past noontime. I looked at my e-mails, chat room calls, faxes and nothing of importance so I went into our living room, plopped down on my chair and wanted to go to sleep but I felt like I just got up!

I heard my beeper go off on my computer and it was an answer (already?) from my employment application this morning. "Sorry, but thank you for your application. However, based on your application and the sources we checked, you are highly overqualified for the position we need to fill. We are seeking someone who just graduated from college programming."

I knew it, and this proved it. Now what am I to do with the rest of my working years?

Just one more thing to put on top of my Anger List! I was so upset I knew I had to just sit, turn on the TV and watch other people's problems as they are a whole lot worse than mine. I was hoping that would slow my mental anguish. On came the news, channel after channel of worldwide news showing plane accidents caused by a pilot vanishing and all aboard perished in the ocean or in a field and many in a neighborhood, train accidents-thousands and thousands of auto accidents on the freeways, busy streets and even in quiet neighborhoods.

It's been a mess in a week's time plus, and it doesn't look like there is light at the end of the tunnel. It seems all the world governments are convening at the UN and giving all its power to them since this vanishing thing is a worldwide event! I turned it off as I thought it would help, but it only made me mentally worse off. I just sat! And before I knew it I was asleep until I heard the phone ring. It was an old buddy of mine checking to see how I was doing and wanted to know if I would be interested in partnering with him on the auctions.

I said, "What auctions?"

He said, "You mean you haven't heard that the UN Authorities have given the go ahead to local authorities to auction off all the homes and businesses that have been left empty. That's the key word-empty. There are no relatives, no partners, no co-stockholders. If it's empty or there are only employees and no owners or if the house is totally vacant, it's going on the auction block. What's owed on the property is what it's being auctioned for, including cars in driveways or garages, furniture, appliances, clothing, all of it for one price, and I understand they are starting to do an inventory of our entire town during the next few days.

They are hiring folks like mad to do this inventory work. Are you interested in partnering on some joint vacant houses or businesses?"

I almost dropped the phone, but I responded with, "Let me think it over and I will call you back in a day or two. Thanks for thinking of me, and how's the family?"

"All are fine on this end. Call me, ok?"

"Ok." I hung up the phone. My immediate thought was of the racquetball club and the house ten houses down, and I thought about all the remaining relatives. Will they gain anything out of this? Who's going to get the money that comes in from the auctions? I thought it was way too soon to start this, but then I thought of all the looting and stealing and the broken windows. Maybe this was a smart thing to do. Time passed faster than I thought as I heard the kids coming in the kitchen door.

And soon I heard the Mrs. drive up and come in the same door, all of them yelled out, "Dad."

I shouted back, "In here."

Soon all our eyes met and naturally they said, "Are you all right Dad?"

"Yep, just kind of being lazy here in my chair."

"Relax, we will help Mom get dinner on. Hope you are hungry."

"Sure am, so call me when all is ready."

"Alright." Thirty minutes later the four of us were at the kitchen table chowing down on another of mom's delicious meals. What a cook she is! Not much talk.

I am sure what happened to me today was no worse or better than what happened to any one of them, but I did ask, "Anybody want to talk about their day?"

And they all shouted at the same time, "No!" Dinner was short. Once again we all helped mom clean up.

It was a Thursday night and before all left to do their own thing for the rest of the night I said, "How would all of you like to invite all of our families over here for Easter celebration and dinner?"

All looked at me with huge smiles and said, "Yes, absolutely, great idea, swell, neat, fantastic, super."

That didn't take much to change our attitudes. All left the kitchen whistling and jumping for joy! The Mrs. said after the kids left, "What gave you this brilliant idea for you know who has to do all the work, but I still like the idea!"

I said, "Well, it's been a number of years since any weddings, births, deaths, and that seems the only time we all congregate so with what's going on with this vanishing thing, I just thought it would be a good idea."

"Sounds great." she said. And after tidying up the kitchen she headed back to our bedroom.

I sat down at the kitchen table and grabbed a pen and piece of paper and started to make a list of those to call to invite with their phone number beside their name. By the list end I had about twenty of us at our home. I figured we could handle that number with kids eating at coffee or end tables. I went back to the bedroom and read the list to the Mrs. and said, "Did I miss anyone?"

She said, "No, but are we going to church that morning?"

I said, "Babe, you know they're all closed!"

She said, "Not necessarily. I heard at the hospital today that the UN is going to demand all churches be open and prepared to receive those who show up for Easter! I overheard that the Jewish church, the Catholics, Baptists, Mormons, and Lutherans, are to be ready by Easter."

I said, "Did you, by any chance, hear who is going to preach or run the service? Didn't all those folks vanish last Wednesday?"

She said, "Not according to what I've heard, only about fifty percent or less vanished from all faiths, but only those faiths that believed in Jesus Christ. None of the others were affected. Anyway that leaves fifty percent still on earth to run the churches and with the help from the UN and other organizations I think it's going to work out. I think by Easter we will have a church to attend. I think and I hope."

47

I said, "Amazing, another item of which I was completely unaware."

Then I said, "Then it's alright if I get on the phone and call all to invite them to our home for Easter, and shall we make it potluck or do we buy everything?"

She yelled back from the bathroom, "Potluck and I will make a list of who's to bring what before I leave for work in the morning."

"Ok," I said. I sat there again stunned by the news she had just shared with me. I thought Fifty percent?

You mean to tell me (I said to myself) that of all those preachers, ministers, priests, rabbis, Sunday school teachers, choir singers, evangelists, missionaries, Christian bookstore people, only fifty percent were left behind! I was boggled! How could fifty percent of those people in their line of work get left behind? Didn't they believe? Didn't they live out their life as a believer? I sat there on the side of my bed once again in a state of total shock. How could this be? How do people who preach this stuff get left out? How do they handle it? It must be a heavy burden on their egos. I mean heavy duty. How are they going to stand up on Easter and tell us to believe when we can blatantly see that they didn't? It's going to be some Easter at church. I can't wait!

Soon the Mrs. came out, crawled in bed and said, "Honey, it's been another exhausting day. Can I say goodnight and go to sleep? Would that bother you?"

"Absolutely not, in fact, let me turn off the light and I will slip into bed also. The kids will know we went to bed." With that it was lights out.

The night went by fast as it always does when one is in a dead sleep. I didn't wake up at 6, but the alarm, thank, God, went off at 6:30 A.M. It's loud enough that the whole family hears it.

I heard one of the kids yell out, "Haven't heard that thing in a long while. Brings back some old memories, Dad."

I kind of chuckled, even at 6:30 A.M. The Mrs. was up. I just laid in bed knowing I had no plans for a Friday, so I just watched her get ready, in fact, she said, "Having fun watching me run around like a chicken?"

I said, "Yes." Soon I could hear the kids heading to the kitchen for a quick bite. The Mrs. hustled out the door for the same. I got up and in my pj's waved to them all as they once again headed out.

I sat at the kitchen table thinking of all my options for the day. It was 9 A.M. The phone rang and it was my friend who called just yesterday about partnering. "Hello."

"Hi, it's me again. I know it's been less than twenty-four hours since I called you, but this auction thing is taking off faster than a bull's eye missile. All the governments are approving it simply because of the rampant looting and there's been a massive amount of rapes in houses where the husband vanished and the wife is alive. I mean it's spooky and the UN wants to stop it by solving it through this method. So what's your thoughts?"

I said, "Let me ask you a few questions since you seem to be really up to date on this subject."

"Fine," he said. "Shoot and I will see if I can answer them."

"First," I said, "How is the government going to take over houses and businesses without actually confiscating them?"

He said, "Eminent domain."

I said, "Ok. Second, what about those who vanished-wills, trusts, estates, bank accounts, checking accounts, debts, family left behind? Who's taking care of all that and life insurance. This is going to break a lot of companies."

He said, "Slow down." Then he said, "First of all wills, trusts, and estates are out the window because no one can show a death certificate and without that no one can prove anyone died! So insurance companies have simply agreed to reimburse all the premiums paid to whoever can prove they are a beneficiary. All debts are cancelled and the company who was owed the debt is out-of-luck. The only folks that are going to get paid are those who can prove a real estate debt, an auto debt or something so that they will get paid off, once the auction sale has passed through escrow.

Let me tell you this. The UN thing has got to be the way to go. They are quick with the solution. So any more questions?"

I said, "How much to buy into this partnership?"

He said, "One hundred thousand dollars."

I said, "Let me mull it over. Call me on Monday."

He said, "Alright," and hung the phone up.

What a predicament! Then I thought what about all the kids and family left by a vanished person, a wife or husband. How are they going to make it? I dialed Star 69 and it redialed my friend. I asked him that question and he said, "Whatever is in the vanished person's portfolio, like bank accounts, stock market, 401K, cash, bank certificate, house, cars, boats, planes, businesses, all of it is going to be put in a holding fund. When all the debts are paid after the auction those who can prove they were the spouse or children or a relative, etc. will get all of the monies less the cost of all the administration work plus any commissions or fees that had to be paid out. I am telling you this is an upright-upscale, money making deal. In the beginning we buy those houses and all that goes with it, turn around and sell all of it for double what we paid for it. It's like taking money from a baby, call me Monday!"

With that I just let out a big Wow! And asked, "Do I want to be involved in something like that?" I said, "I don't think so!!"

I went back and showered and dressed and headed back out to the kitchen, picked up the wife's notes on our Easter dinner and who's to bring what so at almost 11 A.M. I started calling-mom and dad, brother and sister, in-laws, her sister, and I asked them all if they could come and all said yes and then asked them to please bring a dish. I was amazed to catch at least one person home in each family and they spoke for the rest. I invited them all to go to church with us and to be here at 9:30 as church usually started at 10 A.M. That was a job but it was fun as I hadn't actually spoken directly to most of them since Christmas, which was only a little more than three months ago. It was past 1:00 and those two phone calling jobs-the partnering and Easter inviting-were exhausting!

Made myself a bite to eat, turned on my laptop and sent out an e-mail, a note to all the chat rooms I could think of and to the web sites who would be interested in this. Here is what I wrote, "Highly efficient computer programmer with all the credentials you could ask for is seeking employment with a minimum annual wage of $100,000 plus benefits. I am unemployed because of top company management vanishing and company dissolving. E-mail, fax, chat room, or phone me at my home number."

I thought with that I would get a flood, I mean a flood, of inquiries; I shut it down and ate my lunch. About an hour later I got a phone call inquiring about my job memo. I had to move to Iceland to get the job! The Internet is worldwide so I should have expected this kind of call. I said no thanks and hung up. The rest of the day was about as normal as it could be with all that's happening.

Kids were home at the same time, Mrs. home at same time, dinner ready at same time, so all sat down together about the same time. It's Friday night. Lots of folks love to go out for dinner to celebrate going through a week of work, but we always say we're going to go out. We think about it, but we are all so tired it's just easier to stay home and have dinner rather than fight the traffic, then fight the crowd trying to find a table to eat at, then paying a monster price to eat, then fighting traffic to come home. It's easier to stay home. Of course, our meal is better than any restaurant could offer anyway! During dinner, as I always ask if their moods are right, "Well, anything to talk about?"

My daughter spoke up and said, "Don't forget we get out for a whole week before Easter Sunday so next Friday is our last day until the Monday after Easter. In her telling of this upcoming time, I am reminded of our new school nationwide curriculum. It's changed. When I was a kid it was September to June, K to 12. When I graduated from high school or about then the entire nation went to rotation system-school two months, off one month, K-12. Now since my kids started school years back they changed it again. Now the nation has kids go to school year around with a week off for

Christmas and Easter, but now it's K-10th grade. The 10th grade is a kid's senior year. After that they can go on to college or vocational school, which has become very popular.

The reasoning behind this was the school buildings got full use, kids learned faster, and there was no "down-time" for kids to get in trouble. Most kids, it's been found, do go on to college or go to a vocational school so there are less unemployed and less on the welfare rolls. It seems to work! I said, "Yes, we know you both get out for a week but with all that's going on I doubt we will plan on any vacation this year, plus I don't think your mother can get off because of what's going on at the hospital. Right?"

The Mrs. simply nodded yes. Then I said, "Guess what? I got a hold of all the family and all, all will be here, they said, on Easter with a dish and I invited them all to church. So what do you think of that news?" All smiled.

My wife said, "That was nice of you to do honey, thank you."

Soon dinner was over. The kids wanted to go visit a friend a few doors down so that was fine by us. Our daughter is in the ninth grade and our son the tenth. Both are honor students. Both want to go on to college. The Mrs. and I cleaned up the kitchen, went into the living room and fell into our favorite chairs. I said, "Any TV?"

She said, "Not tonight. I am not in the mood to listen to negative news. I hear enough of that all day!"

I said, "OK." We just sat there. It got to be 9:30 sooner than we expected. The kids just walked in. We said we were heading to bed and they said good night. Soon our lights were out and we were asleep without knowing what time the kids called it a night.

Finally, I think got a good night's rest. Woke up at 8 A.M. The sun was up, little breezy as I could see out our bedroom window. The trees were swaying as if they were dancing to a tune of some type. All still asleep, which only means the family is totally exhausted, went into the kitchen, got the O.J., sat at the kitchen table and listened to the wind blew off the rest of the leaves on our trees. Of course, this made all the beautifully kept yards, sidewalks, and streets look as though they hadn't been touched by those caring hands and rakes of homeowners.

Soon the Mrs. walked in and, as always, (still don't know after all these years how she does it), looks great, nothing it seems out of order with her hair, her face, her eyes. She looks as though she hadn't even been to bed and to sleep those last twelve hours. Well, I think it's amazing. She asked if I was hungry and what would I like. I said "yes," and "pancakes with bacon would be great."

She said, "No problem," as she would have said, no matter what I asked for!

The kids walked in and there is a whole other story when it comes to how one looks when they wake up! Told the kids we were having pancakes and bacon. They both yelled out great! They sat and we all watched mom perform her miracle of cooking for all of us.

I said to my daughter, "I hope you are taking lessons from your mom so that someday your family will yell out-great!"

She simply responded, "Dad, yes I am." With that mom served breakfast.

I asked if anyone had any plans on this windy Saturday. Both kids said, "It's the last week before our break at Easter. We are both loaded up with homework so I doubt we will be anywhere but our bedrooms studying."

I turned to the Mrs. and she said, "See this house. I hope all of us can join in to help clean it. It's a mess!"

Naturally I said, "You can count on me." With all finished, I cleaned up and headed to get out of sleepy clothes into Saturday clothes!

While the Mrs. and I were in the bedroom I once again asked her if everything was running smoothly at the hospital and her response was, "It's ok. It's just that it's so hectic seeing all those people filling a huge room that once was filled with kids under seven. So, to be honest, no one at the hospital is in a joyous mood. I mean nurses and doctors are still crying over this vanishing thing. Some doctors came home to empty houses because their spouses vanished. Moms and dads, some now don't have a son or daughter because they vanished. Then all those accident victims laying all over the hospital really add to the chaos. All the staff is burned out and I mean totally exhausted. We are twenty plus people short because they vanished and the administration can't find any qualified people to come in to take up the slack. It's awful and I know it's been tough on you, the kids, and me; I don't know if I have the energy to clean this house today. I am just worn out!"

With that explanation I said to her, "Tell you what. I am filled with enough energy to clean this house so why don't you just take a day off and let me clean! How does that sound?"

"That's awfully sweet! Are you sure?"

"Yes!" With that she crawled back on top of the bed, pulled a cover over her and before I left the room she was back to sleep!

With a promise like I just made I know my day was a done deal. I got out the vacuum, duster, window washer fluid, sink soap, mop, and I headed into it and, to be honest, I had a ball! It's the most laborious work outside of cleaning the yard that I have had to do in, I can't remember, how long. I did every room and hallway in the house except the bedrooms.

The kids both peeked out their doors to ask if they could help and I said, "What, and take all this joy out of me. No. Stay with your homework and then you guys can clean you own rooms."

With that the doors shut and I carried on with my job of joy! The Mrs. never, in all my cleaning and vacuuming noises, opened the bedroom door and I never bothered her. She needed all the rest she could get! By the time I was through, the sun had passed overhead and was on its way to setting. The wind had died to a whisper. The kids had been in their rooms all day, and I just heard the Mrs. coming out of our bedroom. It was almost 4 P.M. and the house was spotless. At least to me it was!

"Honey, what a nice cleaning job you did. Thank you so much for letting me sleep. I really am zonked, so thank you." With that

I walked over and gave her a hug of love and assurance that all was going to be just fine!

She asked if we all would like an early dinner and I said, "Yes but let me check with the kids." They agreed, so she turned her magical wand towards the cupboards, refrigerator, stove and by 5:30, whammo, a meal cooked by a queen!

After dinner everyone was stuffed. The kids asked me a question that I wouldn't have an exact answer for until later on Monday. "Why did some people vanish and the majority of us not vanish. No one seems to have an answer at school, nor is it on the Internet nor have I seen the answer on TV nor in anything I have read! Dad, you seem to always know the answer. What is it? Why and who vanished? Where did they go? And why are we here still?"

And in a laughing way they said, "That's your homework assignment for Monday night!"

I said, "Ok. I will tackle the question." With that we all helped mom clean up the kitchen. The kids said they were about through with their homework. Then they were going to let the TV in their bedrooms put them to sleep. The Mrs., as always, stayed in the kitchen until the last drop of water was dried up! She said she wanted to go on back and go to bed even though it was only 7:30 P.M.

I said, "You do what's best for you!" She did what she said she was going to do.

I went into the living room, turned on the TV. Not much had changed-worldwide- there were pictures of looting, houses burning, businesses being broken into, prisons jammed with guys and gals thinking that because of what had happened they should be let out. Thank God our judicial system is wiser than that. It was awful to watch. I wondered what the kids were going to watch to put them to sleep. Hopefully they will pick out a movie instead of what's actually on TV. Nobody could go to sleep watching that horror! As I watched I wondered why none of that, as far as I know, had happened to our small community. Guess we have just been lucky.

I turned it off and grabbed the local newspaper. Reading, it was almost as bad as TV-gross pictures, gross stories, evil was abounding, but then isn't bad news what sells? I got so I found it difficult to continue to watch all that was going on. I knew it was factual, but I guess I wasn't ready to accept it as real, at least not yet! I thought it was kind of early to go to bed on a Saturday night but life has changed so dramatically that nothing is usual today. I headed on to bed, saying goodnight to the kids as I passed their doors. The Mrs. was already sound asleep. I quietly crawled under the covers and soon the day had passed and a new one was on the horizon.

It was Sunday morning. I had a good night's rest. Normally I remember some parts of some dreams, but not this morning. Heard the kids roaming about. The Mrs. woke up about the same time. It was 8:30 A.M. Oh, that was a good night's rest! Both up and out to the kitchen. She jumped right into breakfast and soon all of us were eating together. I asked the kids if they had checked around at school for the question they had asked me yesterday. They both said that all who were asked were stymied too. The teachers didn't know. The administration had no inkling; even checked the school's Internet and couldn't find a thing about why this vanishing or why only certain ones vanished.

So we ate and, as always, got full, helped clean up as we always do, and I asked everyone what they would like to do today as it was only about 10 A.M. My son said, "Well, I would like to have gone to church this A.M., but the signs "Closed" are still on the church doors. You can see them as we drive by them daily in our bus."

I said, "Well, any other ideas?"

The Mrs. said, "Honey, you have done such a great job in cleaning the entire house. Since you were nice enough to not disturb our bedrooms because of the kids' homework and my sleeping, how about if the three of us clean our rooms and you just sit back and do what you want to do?" I didn't go into the fact that this is what I do all day while they are at school and she at the hospital.

Soon this kitchen was empty. All had shot out to start cleaning their rooms and I was left once again to work out what I was going to do today. I took a shower and dressed, making sure I didn't trip over the vacuum the Mrs. was using. It was just too cold to go out and work in the yard. We have a portable kerosene heater in the garage, so on out to fool around with a bunch of stuff in the garage. I pulled my car out and parked in the driveway, which gave me the whole garage to roam around in, so I did little things-rearranged some shelves, cleaned off the counter and cleaned the working top shelf. I spent most of the day out there just (I hate to say it) doing nothing, just killing time. I knew the family was busy and I didn't want to get in their way. It's 4 P.M. and since we had such a late breakfast, I was famished!

On into the house, the kids were in front of the TV in the living room and I said, "What are you guys watching?"

They said, "Oh, it's all about this vanishing thing and what the new world government is going to do to fix up the world so we can all live in peace!"

I sat down with them and watched. They are proposing a bunch of new ideas, some acceptable but some I didn't like but I didn't want to get into it with the kids. They both are great debaters!

Fortunately just before my mouth was about to open on one of the issues the UN was talking about, the Mrs. called out, "It's dinner time." Saved by the voice of the woman of my life! We all headed to the kitchen table so we could once again enjoy a wonderful meal. She is such a great cook. How could one guy be so lucky!

The rest of the evening went by fast. All wanted to go to bed early to get ready for the last week of school before Easter break and the Mrs. had an idea of what this week at the hospital held for her. By 9:30 all were in bed and soon I followed. It had been a nice day!

I have been sharing with you, the reader, all that I was writing after a thirty-six month oddity in our lives. I have so far given you an almost daily account, but now I will give you, from here on out, highlights of a week, then a month, then a year so that you will know the whole truth of what the world has been like with no hope for tomorrow!)

Chapter Five

"UNITED NATIONS WORLD ORDER"

CHAPTER FIVE

United Nation's New
World Order – NWO

It's Monday morning and soon all said goodbye and were gone. I dreaded today. I would do two things of importance to me. 1) Call the friend who wants me to go into partnership with him, buying up properties where people have vanished — and — I did. I simply told him I wasn't interested and I didn't want to go into all the reasons. He accepted that and that was it. But just to let you know why, I thought it was just plain unethical! I am sure a lot of money is going to be made, but I didn't want any part of it, so that part of my day was finished!

2. The second part of my day was to answer my kids' question as they had asked me to do and I promised to do so by tonight! It got to be afternoon and I thought of ways to find this answer — (A) I went to the big family Bible and opened it. It was as the title said — The King James Edition. I started to look through it, but just its size frightened me and the way it's written is just something I can't catch on to, so closed it. (B) Next was something I figured would have an answer. I searched the Christian Internet and nothing there told me my answer. I thought I did the proper search. (C) I went to the chat room and asked them the question the kids asked and the only response was, "It's in the Bible!" But where?

Not knowing where else to look and not being able to call a church because they are all closed, I decided on (D) to drive down to our local library, walk in and quietly ask the person at the front desk, "Do you have Bibles that speak plain old English and if so can you tell me where to find such a book. I want to know why some people vanished and others didn't? My teenage kids have put this on me as a test and I have to have an answer, if there is such one out there."

She said, "Yes, there are old plain speaking English Bibles

available here in the library and yes, there is an answer to your teenagers' question. You are not the first nor do I expect the last person who has walked through that door asking such a question. In fact, we have had folks steal a Bible or two so we are no longer allowing them to be taken out of the building but you are welcome to sit and read all day if you like. Now, here are the references in the Bible you will want to look up. May I warn you when most people look up these references they don't walk out of here very happy people. In fact, I have seen many weeping as they leave, but here are the references. Go to aisle # four under the heading "Religion." There are several Bibles there. I would choose the one that says, *The New Living Bible.*" It's quite easy to read and comprehend. Good luck and I'm here for any more questions."

With that I walked over to the Religion Section. I found, out of the many, many Bibles on the shelves, the one she recommended, found a chair at a table, pulled out a pen and the library had provided scratch pads to write on, so I began my search. I was spooked over what she said about people leaving weeping? – So — #1 1ˢᵗ Corinthians 6:9 & 10 — First I had to find where the New Testament was I didn't even know there was an old and new – very confusing?

Here is what it said, in a nutshell, "None of these type of people are going to vanish to God's heaven: immoral people, idol worshippers, adulterers, homosexuals, thieves, greedy people, drunks, slanderers, robbers." —Huh! — No wonder only a few million left! And I can't believe one hundred people in our company didn't fall into one of those categories! Wow! If what I just read is true I find it hard to believe anybody vanished! — Anyway – on to the next reference she gave me.

#2 Galatians 5:19-21. Hope there is a bit of hope in this one. – None of these folks will vanish either: those who have impure thoughts, those who seek lustful pleasures, those who worship idols and those who seek demons. Also included are those who hate, who complain, who fight, who are jealous, who display anger, who criticize and those who only look after themselves. None of the following will vanish either; those who feel like the world owes them a living, those who seek wrong doctrine, those who are envious, are murderers, are drunks and those who engage in wild parties. Huh? I couldn't believe what I was reading! Whoever has lived a life without what I have read so far has to be a hermit in Alaska! No way, in these times, can anyone pass this test, no way! But I thought, let's go on.

#3 <u>Ephesians 5:5</u> — none of these folks will vanish: those who are impure, greedy, worship idols, those who love all the toys in life instead of God! So far, three references and all of them say to me that few people went to heaven!

Last one, #4 <u>Revelations 21:27</u> — no one will vanish who's been immoral or dishonest, those were the only four I could find and so it's no wonder folks left here are crying. Who could live a life of such standards? I surely don't know of anyone, and certainly I didn't fit these standards. I was way out of order if this was the life I had to live. I blew it somewhere. I can only blame me, but I did have to ask why didn't someone tell me before March 9th at 3 PM?

I was very confused so I got up and went over to the gal at the information desk and said, "OK, I looked up these four references you gave me, now tell me, who in the world passed this test of living such a life?"

"I don't know sir, but as you can see, you and I are here so I guess we didn't measure up!"

I said, "Is there anything in that book that will tell me exactly who vanished and why them?"

"Yes, look up this verse." So back to the table with pen and paper and I looked up <u>John 3:16</u>. It said, "For God so loved the world that he gave his son so that whoever believed in Him, shall not perish but have everlasting life."

So I wondered what if one believed but didn't live a hermit's life would he vanish? The more I read the more confused I got! I went back to her and asked, "No more questions about what's inside. It's totally put my brain on hold. But since I can't take out a Bible and all the churches are closed and I heard most, if not all, Christian bookstores are closed, where can I find a Bible like that one-easy to read in plain English?"

She said, "Possibly a used book store."

"Thanks." I know of an old bookstore down by our office that I passed a zillion times, so drove to this place, got out of car and went into the store. An elderly man, probably 70+ years and properly dressed said, "Good day, look around. If you need any help just ask me."

I said, "Well I do. Do you have any Bibles, with a name, *The New Living Bible*?"

"We sure have had a lot of requests for such a book and yes, I do have exactly what you want." He went back to the rear of the store, reached up high on a shelf and brought it to me. It looked worn, kind of like that neighbor's Bible, ten houses down our street.

"Ten bucks and it's yours."

I paid him and said thanks and he said as I left, "God bless." Don't recall anyone saying that as a goodbye before?

I drove back to the house, sat down at the kitchen table and went again through all those five places the library gal had given me. I just could not grasp it — live a life of a hermit but believe in the Son of God and you vanish! But then I know that living like a hermit wasn't true because I know one hundred folks at our company didn't live like hermits and no way did the guy who owned that racquetball club live like a hermit. He lived in a million dollar home!

I was so confused I just sat there. In fact, I bowed my head and said, I guess, a prayer. "God if you are really real, then make this book of yours real to me as I am stymied at its content, please." With that, I made lunch for myself. The rest of the day was filled with nothing of importance.

The kids got home, so did the Mrs. At dinner I read to them the notes I had taken down at the library and they and their mother looked at me as if I had lost it somewhere during the day! There only comment was "Sure, Dad."

With that it was another day in our family. The rest of the week was busy but nothing significant happened. I got about four more calls on my e-mail notice of seeking employment. All four would have moved us across the country or to a foreign country, none of which I am willing to do at this time in my life.

On Wednesday at 3 P.M. a lot of folks were still scared to death they would vanish. Far as I could tell based on Wednesday's news reports, no one vanished. The kids got out Friday for a full week for Easter vacation, but with the Mrs. working it doesn't look like we are going anywhere. Besides that with the entire country on the same school curriculum it's almost impossible to find a vacation spot unless you book it a year in advance. It's horrible! The week went by fast as they all do. The Mrs. tells us the hospital situation is worse than ever.

Now, instead of accident victims caused by the vanished non-driven cars, it's now suicide or, at least, attempted suicides. Seems those who vanished and left spouses behind, those left behind are apparently not making it; pills, guns, hangings, alcohol, or drug overdose. She said, you name it, this hospital has seen it and she says based on hospital readouts of what's going on in other hospitals, same type situation. She says the staff is literally exhausted but she has refused to work overtime and they at the hospital have honored that. She is home nightly, like a clock, at 5 P.M.! If she weren't, we three would starve to death!

I did get to the bank and deposit all those checks the company sent and I did rollover the 401K into an IRA. Other than those things it was a quiet week. Oh, I did start reading that $10.00 Bible. Began this time in the new part, can't figure out why they call it new when it's more than two thousand years old. Strange I thought. But so far it's interesting even though God hasn't answered that short prayer about making me understand what I am reading. Now I am reading it in plain language and I still don't grasp it.

The weekend got here and then it was suddenly Monday. Now the Mrs. goes to work and we three sit here wondering what we are going to do on the "vacation week." Of course it's the first time ever that just the three of us are alone as all other times when school is out for Easter and Christmas all four of us go somewhere or do something, but it didn't work out this time. Breakfast is over and I get a phone call from my dad asking if I have a Ouija board and I ask why. He tells me I invited them to church on Easter, but everyone knows all the churches are closed. But he just heard it announced on national TV that the New World Order has told all religions of all faiths that closed their doors to have them open by Easter Sunday and ready to get back to their normal schedule.

So he says, "Tell me how you knew that was going to happen or did you just take a guess at inviting us?"

I said it was a guess and a hope. That was all it was. I told him, "See you guys about 9:45 A.M. in front of that church we go to couple of times a year."

"And thanks for the up-to-date information, bye."

I looked at my kids with a halfway smile and said, "That was your grandpa, and apparently all the churches worldwide are reopening on Easter Sunday."

"Great," both my kids yelled out!

The week went by fast. We took care of our yard work, washed the two cars, and cleaned out the garage. The kids worked on and off on some homework and, if I asked them to help me with something, they obliged. One day they wanted to just go for a ride to maybe go shopping. I suggested that would be great but how about if we also took a ride around and check the status on all those houses and businesses where people vanished and they just sit empty. I hadn't shared with them the partnering phone call that I got.

We left the house and headed west as I wanted to see what was going on with that tenth house from us. And there it was — a sign larger than a regular real estate sign and it said in bold letters, "**THIS PROPERTY AND ALL ITS CONTENTS IS FOR SALE THROUGH THE NEW WORLD ORDER. CONTACT US OR YOUR REAL ESTATE AGENT. NO TRESPASSING**

— PUNISHABLE UNDER WORLD CODE #." Then it gave a couple of phone numbers.

I just sat there in our car looking at this sign and this home. I was in a sticker shock. Soon someone behind me honked and I headed on. I said to the kids, "What do you think of that sign?"

Their response was, "Better than sitting there empty for some robber to come by and steal everything."

"I guess so," was my response. Then I wanted to check one more place so I drove by the racquetball club. In a big, big sign it said the same thing. I got out of my car to go up to the front door. There were no cars in the parking lot. Sign simply said, "CLOSED BY ORDER FROM NEW WORLD ORDER," and have I just paid six months dues!!

I drove the kids to the mall, and based on the traffic, people, and limited parking stalls, you would have thought no one vanished. It was unbelievable, but then Easter is only a few days away. The three of us walked into the mall and all agreed to meet at one place in one hour. They took off. I thought of what direction to go. Amazingly, some stores had the same sign I saw at the racquetball club and our neighbor's house. There weren't too many, but enough that you couldn't miss it. Clothing stores, jewelry stores, hair shops, gadget stores, video stores, and department stores were jammed with people. I wanted to stop at a few of them and get their opinion on the vanishing but I didn't have the nerve to do it. Based on all the scurrying and buying, I hate to say this, but the vanishing was just no big deal. At least not from what I see.

An hour went by fast. Soon the kids were where we agreed to meet and it was out to the car to try to inch our way out without getting in a fender bender. As we drove out they saw their favorite fast food drive thru so we did just that and went on home to eat it at our kitchen table. It was fine but not near as good as the Mrs. cooking! The kids went to visit a friend down the street. I went in and turned on the TV news as usual. I guess, besides telling the religious world to get their act together before Sunday they (the

New World Order) have just about gotten every country to give into the idea of a one-world government. I guess no one had much of a choice.

This new government at the United Nations has the ten largest countries involved, which means they have the largest military backing in the history of mankind. It's nerve racking! So when other countries balk at joining, they probably send them a video of their military power. I am sure after that it's, "Where do we sign?" The only thing that really worries me is <u>total control</u>! So far they have not elected a president or vice president or secretary/treasurer so all ten have one voice and I guess majority wins. It was sad to see our president and vice president resign, but our president is one of the ten, thank God! All countries have to follow suit; our Senate and Congress had the doors closed on them. The New World Order told all countries that states, counties, cities, towns need to work out their problems on a local level. There is no need to spend billions on folks being in New York to make decisions. Each state or local government can make their own decisions and if an issue arises that needs the NWO thoughts or votes then they can bring the issue to them. Sounds a whole lot easier and certainly less expensive.

I guess all our Senators and House of Representatives simply went back to their own states and worked out of their offices there. Sure going to be a lot of empty buildings in Washington, D.C.! But it sounds as if it's a worldwide effort to trim back costs and simplify the way the world is run. Everybody seems to be reacting to all this news without riots or anything like that. Things seem to be running smoothly. The week passed by quickly and the kids found things to do to keep them busy. We (the three of us) did projects together and I really enjoyed their company. As I said before it's been a first for us! The Mrs. worked, cooked, slept, and worked. I feel so terrible (guilty) for not being a working husband, but I am unemployed and hate it!

Before I knew it Easter Sunday was here. We all got up to dress up for church. My Mrs. looked like one of those Hollywood

Queens-what a doll! Mom and Pop came over here so we could all go to church together. I thought we were going to meet them there, but it's fine since it's mom and dad. Had a quick, not-big, breakfast and the six of us were off to the open church with folks preaching who didn't get vanished! The parking lot was full, but we found a space. It reminded me of the mall/crowded! Into the church, music was playing; a choir of about twenty folks was up on the podium. I recall it to be just that many before the vanishing. We found a pew that seated all six of us. Soon the, I guess, preacher came up to the podium, the music stopped and he started. He spoke for about forty-five minutes, most of it was an Easter message. He spoke very little about the vanishing probably because he wasn't vanished. There was more music and we sang a couple of songs. Prayers were given. Normally they took a plate and passed it around. I put in my normal five-dollar bill. I didn't look to see if Pop put money in the plate. In about an hour and fifteen minutes it was over and out to our car we went. I was disappointed in the fact that he didn't tell us, who are left, what we are supposed to do or what to look forward to. In regards to that I wasn't happy!

We went back to the house. It was almost noon and the rest of the family started walking in and by 1:30 everybody was here. All brought a "potluck dish"! All found a chair. The kids thought it was neat that everybody showed up. Usually at least someone calls and says can't make it-sorry! But not this time! The Mrs. with the help of all the other gals made a fabulous dinner. We guys all sat out in the living room talking about a million things. Of course, the number one subject was the New World Order. Sadly most of it was negative, of which I was surprised as I thought it all sounded reasonable. Their concern was "sooner than we think this group of individuals is going to be controlling our lives much more than anybody suspects."

Soon the call, "Dinner's ready" came out and the food was served. The adults sat at the dining room table (which we only sit at maybe two times a year) and the kids sat at the kitchen table.

Somebody asked if anyone was going to pray over the food on

the table. No one spoke up so I said, "Yes, I will" and I was stymied at what to say so I said a quick prayer to whoever God is and said, "Help."

"Dear God bless this food sitting before us and thank you for church this morning. Thank you for all the blessings you have given to us and we sure do ask you in some way to tell us what we have to look forward to after this vanishing thing. Thank you and Amen."

We all opened our eyes and they were gazing at me and about half of them at the table said, "Where did you learn to pray?"

I didn't respond. We sat and dinner was served. We ate, we laughed, we even cried a few times. We chitchatted, and forty-five minutes later, the gals were cleaning up and once again we guys were discussing the world situation. It seemed like the day went by way too fast. Folks were saying goodbye and see you at Christmas or Thanksgiving. Before we knew it, all had left and we all four agreed this was a good Easter day. We all jumped in and helped clean up and put everything back the way it was. It got to be 9 P.M. and all headed to do what needed to be done to get a good night's rest before our regular schedules began tomorrow at 6:30 A.M.

Another week home alone. No calls other than from foreign countries came in on my job applying. I decided to do what I said I wouldn't do, start my own company in computer programming. I spent the whole week working on the perfect website and e-mail program.

Besides that, the sale of homes and businesses that were empty via the vanishing went on the auction block April 1st. It can be bought via the Internet, at auction houses set up in each major city in each state, or through a realtor. None of it was done at the actual site and, I guess, that was good. There would be too many rubberneckers, gawkers, and tire kickers. This eliminates all of that and, from what I have seen so far, a person could actually see what they were bidding on because the NWO had each site videotaped. If interested in an area worldwide, you could select that area, what price you want to pay, and punch in a number-Bingo-the video came up of that property. Kind of slick, I thought!

I still don't think it's equitable to those left behind who would have inherited if the folks that owned the property had died instead of vanished, but who am I to say? Also, I don't think it's ethical! I am still glad with my decision to not get involved partnering, but it could be a bonanza for those who go after those properties. I just hope the tenth house down sells to a nice family who keeps up the yard and house like the rest of us do. Of course, I also wondered if my 6 + months dues I paid at the club would be honored by the new owners, whoever took over.

The other thing I did this week in regards to the properties being auctioned, was to drive to just do some comparing. I want to see how many homes in the exclusive neighborhoods were on the auction block versus the poorer neighborhoods. We don't have a whole lot of poor folks in this town, I don't think. So off I went to do my secret little comparison. First I went to a couple of exclusive areas I know. I drove kind of slow but not so slow folks would think I was casing the neighborhood. I had to get past a security guard gate at each neighborhood but being a computer programmer it wasn't tough to figure out their codes. I was amazed. In both neighborhoods I only counted <u>five</u> houses with auction signs, out of probably, I'm guessing, three hundred, maybe five hundred houses. I am sure I missed maybe a few blocks. But, even so, that number was astounding.

Then I drove to what was considered our poor, low-income neighborhood. It didn't take long to see the numerous auction signs. One out of five, I counted fifty and quit! Of course, I asked myself why such a vast difference and the only conclusion I could remotely come up with was, "The rich depend on their money to get them through life and the poor depend on God to get them through life." It's the only reasoning I could muster up. Otherwise why else would there be such a vast difference in houses being auctioned? I guess those were the highlights.

Then kids went back to school. The Mrs. worked at the hospital.

She says suicides have more than doubled since she last spoke of it. It just has the police department, fire department, suicide prevention people, coroner's office, mortuaries, and the hospital over worked, over exhausted and there is not a light at the end of the tunnel in this situation. What a tragedy! The weekend got here. The Mrs. said she was so exhausted she asked if we could clean up the house and even, if we would cook for ourselves. We all said ok knowing how tired and overworked she is feeling. Saturday, Sunday and before I knew it we were into April and all seemed to be about as normal, in our house, as it was before the vanishing.

This next week was not so great. It stormed and no one knows why, but crops, orchards, fields, plants, things that grow food seemed to gotten some kind of disease and it's killing off the world's food supply. Even those massive bins and storage units that hold food and those high refrigerator plants that hold meat and vegetables have all been affected and to make matters worse a disease has affected the livestock all over the world. I remember that mad-cow stuff, way back when I was a kid. The only hope is for scientists to figure out a solution to remedy it. They probably will but in the meantime massive amounts of food that would have been available are dying out. There are still 7 billion people left on earth so it takes a lot of food to feed us all! I guess the NWO will figure something out, that's their job now!

Also, on the good side, I got several inquiries on my website and I have gotten a few jobs to do. I had to go down to the computer store to buy some updated equipment to handle this influx of work, but I got it all set up in a spare room. I have now made it my office. It had been the family junk room! So on the positive side this has worked out so that I will be providing an income, which I hope will throw that guilt feeling out the window.

Another week has come and gone. This next week was income tax week, leading up to that infamous day, April 15th. I wondered how they, the IRS, were going to deal with those taxes due or refunds to those that vanished. It took me all week, but I got them completed. I am not getting anything back but don't owe very much either, so that's good! By the fourteenth I had the Mrs. signed our tax form and mailed it off. There was nothing of significance that happened in the remainder of April. To those reading this, there is nothing more to discuss in this report.

Chapter Six

"THE PILL"

CHAPTER SIX
"The Pill"

May got here and it was not a good month! In fact of all the writing I have done thus far this is by far the worst to affect our lives. Perhaps the worst in the history of mankind. Here is what happened – The scientists of the entire world, all that brain power and computer power have <u>not</u> been able to completely stop the disease set upon the human race. The food supply and the food that is/was available is dwindling sharply, so, the NWO has decided to install a voluntary Death Pill! It's mainly designed for just a few classes among the living:

1) For the pet and zoo population. (Thank God we don't have a cat or dog!)
2) For the elderly over 75 years age. (Apparently the NWO feels those folks are nonproductive.)
3) For the mentally ill and disabled who can't work.
4) For the blind, deaf, mute.

The figure in a report I read states that if those above were to take the death pill that would eliminate at least a billion people and the pets. I don't think this idea is going to work especially if it's on a volunteer basis. So far that's the worst news I have ever seen in all of my years! I have no idea how they are going to implement it but just have to wait to see what happens. That was the first part of May. By May 20th it went from volunteering to mandatory, simply because no one could develop a solution to the problem of the world's diminishing food supply. In fact, at this time, end of May, the world's ocean sea life has also been affected to make matters a thousand percent worse than what they were.

The kids are frantic over it as it's the only thing they discuss on campus. My Mrs. says the hospital is against the death pill as it's inhuman and ungodly. And they don't know how they are going to handle the situation based on hospital and staff availability. It's the absolute worst mess I have ever seen. The vanishing hardly affected people after a month or so. This is going to put the entire world in chaos. But I don't know what else those ten folks can do (NWO organization). What other options do they have? The world is in chaos over this food situation and to this day, almost the end of May, not one person has come up with an idea for a solution. I went back to my notes that I jotted down from Matthew 24. I wrote down 29 different things that are supposed to happen and based on what I read this is surely, in my opinion one of them.

By June the food supply was worse than ever and fortunately (don't know why?) but our tiny community hasn't been hit nearly as badly as you see on TV. I mean people in other parts of the world are fighting over any kind of food to put in their stomachs. The NWO is trying to keep calm but it's tough. They have ambassadors in each country. Then it's the old domino theory trickling down so that a rule/law is made, it's passed to this ambassador, then to the senator/congress person, then to folks below them and then it, in some way, affects us. Also they have not given out the death pill as yet. There was too much backlash from lots of people. I am assuming that they are waiting until the last moment. I did see that NWO had demanded that this pill only be administered by a doctor and that the person who was taking the pill had gotten their affairs one hundred percent in order, including the place of eternal rest (a grave or cremation?) It all sounds so unreasonable. To be honest, with what's going on regarding this diseased food, I don't know of any other option. I guess, it sounds right that those who cannot work or be of value to the world have to make room for those that can still be of value. It's really spooky!

June went by fast. Summer is on the horizon and from what I see and hear no one is sure how long the human race will last. It took till almost the end of July to, I guess, get to its worst point in this food situation. They have somewhat stopped it with some kind of solution they spray over the crops via a plane, but it's not going to do any good for what's been harvested or picked and put away. Most of all that food had to be burned or buried and multi-millions of animals had to be buried in massive bulldozed graves, as the disease couldn't be reversed. Government, schools, grocery stores, hospitals, the militaries, the poor, restaurants, fast foods and the rich are all in the same boat. There just isn't enough food to go around.

They decided that on August first (The NWO) would implement the death pill on a voluntary basis. I kept asking, who's going to volunteer to die or give up their pet to die. No one I knew! Fortunately the Mrs. and my parents are all under seventy-five years of age, and for some reason, I can't think of anyone in the family that has a pet dog or cat. August first got here, apparently the NWO was expecting massive crowds to be at the front door of their doctor's office or at a hospital or qualified medical clinic where someone could also administer the pill, but it didn't happen. A few of the mentally ill showed up. A few dear souls came with their pets (probably sick anyway), but all in all it was a bust. No one wanted to die! But the NWO knew they had to do something about this food disaster. And if the solution they sprayed on the plants and trees that provided food was going to work, it wouldn't be until next year that a new non-diseased supply of food would be ready! There apparently is <u>not</u> enough food to go around even as I write! So it's a waiting game.

In the middle of August NWO came out and said it's no longer voluntary, it's mandatory! My business has picked up substantially. I get about one request in a day to do a program, and that keeps me busy and based on the prices I am charging it almost equals what I was making at the company I worked for. The kids are maintaining a 4.0 even in the midst of all this horror going on. We still have dinner about 5:30 each night. The Mrs. finds ways to cook what's available in the house. The store shelves are not what they used to be. Fruit, and vegetables are not nearly as available. Most is slim picking. Breads are almost empty on the shelves. The only milk available is in cans. In fact, most of everything in all the stores is in cans. It's the only way to eat safely. What a difference from the way we were living just about <u>six months ago</u>, and if it keeps going like this, who knows what the future holds for all mankind. (Was just thinking how lucky those folks are who vanished, not to be able to see what life is like now!)

We are just starting September. The 9th of the month came up and lots of people thought for sure on that day at 3 P.M. there would be another vanishing as it's been six months. It didn't happen! About the best thing that's happened to me individually is I have really taken an interest in this $10.00 Bible I bought at that used book store. I have read the books of the guys who walked with Jesus. I read the story of Acts and how Paul came into the picture and I read Romans, which is a long letter to, I guess, the Jewish people who didn't believe that Jesus Christ was the Messiah. My only regret is not reading this long before the age I am now, and I guess I regret my mom and dad and her mom and dad not getting involved in a church life so that we could have learned from them. But, as the Mrs. always says, "That's water under the bridge." I am noticing that this book I am reading is starting to make a little sense, but I am mystified by so many things and it happened way over two thousand years ago so parts of it are difficult to believe. I guess that's where faith comes in?

The NWO has put off the mandatory death pill and said it would still work on the voluntary basis until "Further Notice." They have now in <u>six months</u> been able to really get organized. They say Washington, D.C. is like a ghost city now that all the politicians have been sent back to their respective states. That's got to be a massive savings in tax dollars spent. I am, as well as most folks interviewed are, astonished how this NWO took over so rapidly and so efficiently. It was almost as if this is something that's been sitting on a shelf ready to be taken down in the case of such as the vanishings. The agreement to let these ten government people (ours being one of the ten/the president of the USA), another the prime minister of Canada, another the president of Mexico and the president of Russia and the premier of China and the heads of the other five biggest countries. It's just almost too hard to believe the world now has:

1) one government
2) one military
3) one utility
4) one food distribution
5) one oil and gas distribution and a whole lot of power! The world, I guess, had to come to this. There was already too much chaos worldwide and when the vanishing hit it just quadrupled the chaos. I have read they are working on:
6) one universal language to be taught (I heard it's going to be English.)
7) one monetary system. You will have to have some type of I.D. to buy-sell-work-etc.
8) and a mandatory birth control system (one child per couple maximum).

It's kind of scary, but on the other hand, it's kind of refreshing. (I guess?)

We are going into October. The old leaves are turning fall colors. The kids are doing great. The Mrs. needs a long vacation, but due to school, her job, what's going on in the world and my new company just getting off the ground, we just can't take one. Back in my days we used to celebrate the day/night called Halloween, but back when our kids were babies the government decided to take it off the calendar. It was never a legal holiday, but it was a kid thing. Well, too many bad things happened in the years prior to them stopping it. There was lots of devil type stuff and there were child kidnappings and a bunch of killings and a whole lot of kids landed up in the hospital over twisted people putting poison in whatever they gave out to the kids. It got bad. So from Easter to Thanksgiving not much happens holiday wise. But thankfully, Thanksgiving is less than two months away. Of course, most folks are going to wonder what they are supposed to be thankful for knowing all the misery going on worldwide!

There are so many things that I haven't even talked about in this note. If I were to mention all the daily changes going on in the world there would not be enough pen and paper nor would you be able to finish this report. The end of this report is not far away. Don't forget that I told you I was writing this information thirty-six months after the vanishings. So let's go on.

It is the end of October and fall is upon us. It has cooled down considerably. We are beginning to wear heavier clothing. The air conditioners are off and the gas/oil heaters are on. The kids are really looking forward to Thanksgiving. They don't get any school time off except the Thursday, which is Thanksgiving Day and then that Friday. The Mrs. gets Thanksgiving off because of her seniority. Me-I am self-employed and according to my family-I get every day off! And to be honest-had I known I could make an income having a website selling my own services I probably would have done it years ago, but I was comfortable where I was. I enjoyed the camaraderie and the company paid me well for what I did. Had the vanishing not come along, I would still be there to this day! The house and racquetball club sold to whomever; I haven't the faintest. The food situation has eased but they are still asking for volunteers to accept the death pill if you fell into one of <u>those</u> classes I described before and still not many have taken the NWO up on their offer!

Our utility bills have gone up considerably and I was told it was because the rich countries, like the USA, has to share with all the poor countries because now we are under one big government. Our auto gas cost has gone up, food prices have sky rocketed. The biggest thing that has shown a dive in sales is the entertainment world. No one has the money for anything more than a rented video once in a while and it's not like the old days when you went to a store and rented like I used to do. This renting a video via the TV came online about ten years ago and just about every movie rental store shut their doors! I said, "Why go out and rent when you can rent on your TV with a push of a button!" It's all computerized and you get your bill at the end of a month. So far it's gone over gangbusters. With the food disease and the fact that it is only safe to eat canned food, most folks are staying home. This has caused major bankruptcies in the restaurant business, worldwide!

October and November went by. During those two months the auctioning of homes and businesses went better than expected, but from what I read, a lot of folks who expected money from those that vanished, didn't end up getting much of what they probably should have gotten. The NWO allowed lots of cost to be included and they sold them so cheap that it was just to get one more problem quickly solved! It was a sorrowful thing to see, but the NWO didn't have much choice.

This was supposed to have been an election year for a whole lot of politicians, but the NWO put on hold all elections in all the countries all over the world. They, the NWO, said they wanted experienced people to stay in office until they felt comfortable to make any further changes. This again made sound sense, and it stopped us from having to once again vote via the Internet or from our TV. It beats the old way of voting, (going to a polling place and standing in some person's garage waiting my turn to vote; it was crazy.) Now we vote right in our own houses! It's like our schooling today. Parents have options-1) you can send your children to a public school, 2) you can send your children to a private school and take a full tax donation on the total cost, and 3) you can keep your children at home, get lessons via the Internet or a home schooling program on TV and take a full donation for any cost expended. About 60 percent send to public school, with the other forty divided between private and home schooling. We let our children go to public schools because that's the way we were brought up and we felt if it was good enough for us, it's got to be good enough for them.

Thanksgiving arrived. We had my mom and dad over. The kids got out of school for two days. The Mrs. did a fabulous job. The only problem worldwide in those countries that celebrate this time of year was there were no turkeys! None! They all had to be killed because when they were just being born along with the older turkeys they <u>all</u> got the disease that affected so many other edible animals. But we managed with all kinds of different canned foods, and as I have mentioned, the Mrs. is a magician in the kitchen. So all in all Thanksgiving was good. Christmas is less than a month away. It's getting much colder and we have had some rain. Kids are looking forward to a Christmas break and the Mrs. is applying for a few days off at Christmas time.

The NWO has instituted worldwide a flat tax of ten percent on all that is sold everywhere. They are eliminating all other taxes worldwide. No more income tax, inheritance tax, license tax, food tax nor do we get to write anything off, no more 1040s-1099s, W-2s, nothing! All countries by January first must have in place this new tax code. If not, stiff fines will be put on countries that don't comply. Most of the world is complying. If some don't, a special unit goes out from the NWO and they are tough from what I hear and I guess after a visit from them, they comply. Anyway this will do away with the IRS whom no one has liked since I was a little kid and heard my dad yelling at them! So I guess whatever we buy-property, food, merchandise, a trip, gasoline, utilities, doesn't matter what it is, if you buy it, you pay a ten percent tax and that tax goes directly to the NWO. They then distribute it to where it needs to go throughout the world. Sounds sensible to me. That means I only have this last year to do this miserable tax form. It's over, come April 15th. Best news I have had in many a day!

With Christmas just a short time away we as a family started going to church on a regular basis. I'm reading this Bible I bought and I am into the letters Paul wrote to all those different churches or individuals. I guess my short prayer to God about helping me understand what I am reading is being answered because the more I read and reread the more I am getting to understand what Christianity is about. I am, however, still a long way from saying I am a Christian! I have met some folks at church, but the few old timers won't discuss the vanishing and I guess the only reason is they are embarrassed that they didn't get vanished. Also Christmas trees are out in front of stores. It doesn't bear any food so it wasn't touched by that disease that took most of the foods bearing trees and plants worldwide.

On a Saturday, around mid-December, the four of us went tree hunting. We found one at a Christmas tree lot down by the coffee shop I go to every once in a while. Took it home and decorated it. We did a great job and set it where we always do-right in front of our living room bay window that looks out to our front yard and our neighborhood street. Before we knew it Christmas was here. The kids got out of school for about ten days and the Mrs. got her wish-a five-day vacation reprieve from the hospital that has literally worn her to a frazzle. I had gone shopping at our favorite mall to buy the kids a few gifts, got the Mrs. some perfume and what she wanted-a new king-size bed cover. Expensive but that's what she wanted. Got mom and dad a gift and that was my shopping spree. Vacation got here and Christmas got here. The four of us went to the Mrs.'s mom and dad's for a big Christmas dinner, but no turkey, just none available! Her mom is a good, if not better, cook than the Mrs. We had a wonderful meal, and in addition to this, it was the first Christmas, at least in my lifetime, that we knew the real meaning of Christmas-Jesus Christ, his birth, the three wise men, and the manger!

I thought, all my life, that it was just some storybook fairytale, but after pouring through the Bible as I have been doing I now have come to this conclusion-it's not a fairytale. It's a fact that I hope now I come to believe by faith since God has opened up my mind as to what's written on those pages. I never thought that this would have happened to me as I have said I was the big bang believer, but I guess God had a different plan for me! There were lots of laughs and chitchat and a time to exchange gifts and take a full roll of pictures. We were home by 8:00. The rest of Christmas went by fast and New Year's was upon us.

We aren't ones to do anything outside the house except stay up until midnight and watch how the world brings in a new year via our TV. It didn't seem quite as joyous as in past years and I can understand. Lots of folks are missing a parent, a child, a baby that never got taken home from the hospital and it has caused distress to those who are still here on earth. Then the death pill has people all over the world terribly afraid as NWO is going to make it mandatory soon. Anyway in looking back over the last twelve months it hasn't been bad for us. In fact, as I said at Christmas dinner we all have a lot to be thankful for despite all that is going on worldwide. After thinking about it, all agreed, even our kids!

Can't believe it, but the New Year is upon us! My business has doubled since I started it via a website and emails just a few months back. In fact, it kept me busy more than an eight-hour workday, but I am enjoying it very much. January 1st was D-Day for taxes and yes, it feels so good that never, after April 15th, will I have to even give a thought to these tax forms or the IRS! Kids are back in school. Our son only has until June and then he graduates from high school and moves on to college (and that's expensive-hundred thousand a year and that's just tuition.) He is planning on going to our local college so he will live here at the house. The Mrs. went back to work full of pep and zest. Hope she stays as upbeat as she was through Christmas break. She was really positive for being in such a negative place at work! The first week of January went by being very, very cold all over the world! There have been extraordinary amounts of snow and our temperatures are below normal levels. It's difficult just to go out to pick up the A.M. newspaper!

It was the ninth of January when the world found out it was in for some major changes in the history books of mankind and anyone who had even opened the Bible knew this was foretold thousands of years back. It shook the foundation of humanity! Here's what happened: The NWO after now nine months of swaying back and forth on the death pill decided it was to be mandatory effective immediately. It gave the world three months to comply.

Otherwise those who were being mandated would be in violation and they would be gathered up and forced to take the pill. They had by now developed a serum so it could be taken by vaccination. This was an option especially for the pet world. It had people committing suicide by the millions all over the world, but it also, according to reports, had families trying to hide their parents or in-laws or anyone over age 75 or a mentally retarded child or a handicapped person. It was the worst case of hysteria I have seen in my life. The daily newspapers had huge letters as I had never seen before! <u>SUICIDES!</u> Then another <u>DEATH WISH!</u> And another <u>MILLIONS DIE!</u> It was enough to shake the strongest of persons.

By March 9th it's estimated that about a billion people on earth dead, not including an enormous amount of animals worldwide! The "<u>only</u>" reason for all this is simple. There just isn't enough food to feed seven billion people! So a hard, difficult decision had to be made. "Who is to be eliminated?" Thank God, I didn't have to be part of that decision-making! Just think of the most horrible thing you have ever seen or heard about, and then quadruple it. That's what's going on in present day humanity! That's the worst of all I am going to share in terms of what the NWO has instituted as laws to be enforced from the ninth day of January forward.

Now here is the list of what happened next and it was harsh but it was the only way to save our humanity. The solution to bringing back life to the trees and bush food supply had not worked out as planned. It seems no matter what part of earth they tried to re-plant it just wasn't working-Africa, Cuba, Mexico, Hawaii, Asia, China, Russia, all through Europe, Canada, USA, and all the weather zones. The soil differences-it just wouldn't take hold and grow. It's like someone poisoned earth and nothing planted would grow to any food value! In addition no matter how the scientists have tried different sperms on animals they wouldn't conceive and so the cow, horse, chicken, turkey, lamb are almost extinct because it's been found an impossibility to get then to reproduce.

It's so spooky I have a difficult time even writing about it but someone has to know what trials mankind has been through! Add to this that not only were the over age 75 required to take the pill along with the mentally ill, blind, deaf, and disabled, but the entire pet and zoo animal population and even the wild life were too! Now they added the prisoners in jail. If they were a convicted killer, rapist, gang related, or any other violent crime they had until March 9th to take the pill or injection. Then they added all those in nursing homes! The NWO did allow folks to take the pill at home so the family could be there versus the original plan where it had to be done at a doctor's office or hospital. Now one can go get the pill at a pharmacy, doctor's office, hospital, but one must fill out a long form indicating one has set their affairs in order and it must be signed by a person where the pill or injection was dispensed.

It's driving people to the point of just outright suicide or trying to run away! But where can one run to now that the world is like one big community?

1) <u>Food Rationing</u> All humanity was given coupons to buy food. Once you used up your coupons, you better have food left over in your cupboard or home. Money was of no value (except on the black market as there were always stories on the news of people stealing food then selling it for massive profits)! It was difficult but as a family we seemed to manage OK.

2) <u>Utility Rationing</u> This came about as a result of severe coldness that had swept the earth. It's like a cold wave came out of the heavens and stopped on planet earth-oil, fuel, gas had to be searched for even farther down into the earth than ever before. Rivers and lakes and some smaller oceans have frozen over worldwide. Someone suggested the earth is returning to the Ice Age. Our rationing was to use seventy-five percent of what was used last year. If you used more than that or tried to, you were cut off. It's all computerized

so it's difficult to cheat. Warm blankets and heavy clothing were a standard all over the world.

3) <u>Auto, truck, farming, equipment, trains, planes, fuel rationing</u> All went to rationing. This rationing was the same scenario as above. We got seventy-five percent of fuel that we had used last year to use now. So if I used one thousand gallons of gas last year, the <u>maximum</u> I can buy this year is seven hundred fifty. This again brought on the black market trade and again it showed pictures of police catching thieves trying to steal gas and oil to sell for a big profit! One just drove less, went less, and of course, this hurt countless businesses, as people would save up for an emergency or for getting to work. One didn't fool around with this rationing, nor did they with the food or utilities!

4) <u>Crime Deterrent</u> You would think that people would not commit crimes during this worldwide crises, but it seems to be worse than ever! Murder, gangs more than ever, rape is rampant, worldwide theft is up ten thousand percent and a whole list of crimes that would take up too much space to list. It seems according the NWO that the only way to deter crime is to force those found guilty to take the death pill. But it seems that hasn't stopped the evilness that is rampant worldwide. The NWO has abolished the Jury System Worldwide. It has given judges already appointed before the day of vanishing the authority to pass judgment on those brought before them. There is no more appealing a judge's decision. Once it's decided, it's as solid as cement.

The less than violent criminals are put in prisons throughout the world but there is no more hanky-panky. It's working while they are doing their time. They have decided to make going to prison extremely uncomfortable! No more are prisons home for violent criminals, now it's a pauper's grave! Also if a criminal committed a crime anywhere on earth, it was the same punishment worldwide.

They canceled such things as extradition or the work escape. One could not escape unless one had a spaceship to get off the planet. Violent criminals knew if they got caught and a judge found them guilty there was no way out. It was over for them, regardless of age! No more juvenile crimes! All criminals were treated equally, but sadly, it didn't put a stop to criminal activity, it just got worse!

5) <u>One World Language</u> It was decided by the NWO that the world needed to have one language and so it ordered the world community to have the English language as its major language within the next twenty-four months. The world could keep whatever language it spoke as a secondary language but the NWO wanted one language so that the world of humanity no matter where could communicate! Books, teachers, videos, CD's/DVD's, the Internet, even movie theaters were giving, showing how to speak the English language. It went over but a lot of people in many countries balked at it. It was however soon to be known as law and we all had to get used to it.

6) <u>Child Bearing</u> Because there are seven billion people on earth, the NWO has demanded that no more than one child could be born to a family. Those that have children, eight to whatever age could keep them. (Remember all those on March 9, last year, seven years of age or younger vanished so there were no small children or babies worldwide!) If a couple or a single mother had more than one child, the second child was given to a family that was childless. There is lots of hysteria over this new world order law, but how are/is the world going to feed them? It was difficult to accept but when no alternatives were put forth it was simply accepted. Of course, people decided worldwide to consent because people basically said, "Who wants to bring a child into this kind of world." That was, even in my opinion, a true statement!

7) <u>Everybody Works</u> Bottom line was if you didn't have a job, the NWO told the countries to find them one! There was no longer to be welfare, unemployment, Food Stamps, etc.-you work or you starve and no one enjoyed being hungry! We would drive to the store or mall or to church and you would see men and women working doing all sorts of stuff. It was a first for me to see this, but I thought it was good as I was one of those who didn't believe in a free handout for folks who could do a day's job! Also the law stated that if one didn't work, one got zero rationing! That put everybody on alert! Including me, but I could prove I worked even though I did it from my house. If anyone were to ask for proof all I had to do was show the form asking for computer programming and the check I received for doing such work!

8) <u>Air Pollution Standards</u> This was a law that had to be enforced. The blocking of the sun's rays was of great concern from years ago and it's just gotten worse. Some say it's what's led to this year's worldwide coldness. The sun simply can't get through to warm the planet. Also many scientists say it's what contributed to the disease that killed all the trees and bush plants that fed the world. That also affected the killing of the animals the world used to eat and those in the oceanic world say the waters have warmed up too much because of what's going on worldwide and that's caused the demise of billions upon billions of fish the world used to have as food! It's a major disaster worldwide, but the NWO say there is hope if we will all abide by the eight rules set upon humanity. These pollution rules apply to all manufacturing, auto smog, tobacco industry, the oil industry and any industry whereby fumes or smoke went up into air. Most folks I talked to were in total agreement on this last law given out by the NWO!

Well, that was it. Those eight new worldwide laws were on TV, the Internet, published in every newspaper in every language on the face of the earth. Of course, it was the old story of, "So you got a law, who's going to enforce it?" But with the rule regarding everybody working (#7) it just may be that the NWO will be able to apply the power to enforce those eight new laws. Only time will tell.

January flew by. Not much change in our home even with all the rationing and death pill and crime. Happy to say none of it at least seemed to affect us very much. We had heat in the house, gas for our two cars, the kids went back and forth to school. The Mrs.'s job at the hospital is terrible (her exact word) and I am doing well in my programming business so all in all even with all the world's problems you would never know it by our or our neighbors' lifestyles!

One major thing I decided to do in January is to become a Christian. I have read this Bible enough to know if I am going to live out this life I want it to be with God in control. Yes my life has been good. We have never gone without, but that can't be the sum total of living-just having a nice home, a good career, a loving spouse, two great kids, a supportive family, two cars, and a garage full of stuff we don't need anymore. If you add all that up what does it total? It totals the average life, at least here in the USA. But it must not be good enough for God. Otherwise, I would have been one of the hundred million plus people that vanished. After nine months they finally estimated that was the sum total that left planet earth via God on March 9th last year so when I added up my years and all my possessions, I figured, in God's eyes it added up to zero! So I had to make a change.

The Bible gave us the tools to do so. I didn't go to a church to do what I now needed to do. The messages on Sundays were good but I kept asking myself why those who were preaching were still here. Why didn't they vanish? Why did God leave them out of his plan? So even though I went (occasionally) to church I thought it best if I confessed my past to God, all my errors, wrongs, and mistakes. So, in our bedroom on my knees, I asked Him to take over me.

Then I went into our bathroom, made a hot tub of water, got into it fully clothed and I baptized myself as it said we should do in the Bible. To be totally honest, when my head came up out of the water in that bathtub I felt this, hard to describe, wonderful feeling. For reasons I can't explain God was present in that bathroom. I know I am losing it, but again it was just weird how I felt. It was just sooo gooood! That's about the best I can do to tell you the feeling. I told the kids and the Mrs. what I had done and they, of course, didn't understand no matter how much I explained. I told them that what I got they could have. The Bible was on the kitchen table. Anyone could read it like I did!

February went by and another massive announcement came. For the first time in the history of mankind there would be a worldwide holiday. Everything shuts down on March 9th to remember those who vanished one year ago. They named the day "Mourning Day" a day to mourn over those taken by God. I thought it should be the opposite as it should be to celebrate their victory and mourn for us who didn't vanish, but who am I. When the day got here (it was a Friday this year) the world's wheels of commerce, entertainment, socializing, work of any kind came to a halt. In fact the NWO stated in its Proclamation that at 3 P.M., the moment all hundred million (estimated) vanished we should literally stop in our tracks no matter where we were and give thought to those who are no longer here. Friday, the 9th arrived.

Chapter Seven

"ONE YEAR HAS PASSED"

CHAPTER SEVEN
"One Year Has Passed"

The Mrs. stayed home! The schools worldwide shut their doors so the kids went home. It was too cold to go out and do anything so we just kind of sat around. At 3 P.M. they had church bells ringing all over the place. In our town we have two churches with big steeples with bells. They rang and rang, probably for at least five minutes plus at 3 P.M. It was an awesome sight on TV. People were openly crying on streets all over the world, remembering those that vanished and those who are having to take the death pill. It got so sad the Mrs. and I sat in our living room bawling our eyes out over what was being shown on TV. It was a sad, sad day across the world, but like every day, it passed. The rest of March came and went.

April got here and I was so happy to see the 15th come and no IRS, no 1040s, no deductions, no hours poring over paper work, no 1099s, no nothing! All taxes are now paid in the simplest form ever. It's in anything one buys-heat, oil, gas, food, clothing, auto purchases, you name it, if you buy it, you pay a tax. Hard to believe we didn't do this a hundred years ago! Based on what I have read there has been little corruption and there has been enough coming in to the NWO so that no one on the planet gets less or more than they need. In other words, the tax collected is being fairly distributed worldwide. I think that's amazing!

April left like a cold wind blew into town and, as fast as it blew in, it blew out. May got here, the weather warmed up, the flowers began to bloom, the grass began to look like it needed mowing, the trees looked as if they had been through a rough storm, but they survived it and the blooms on them were starting to show their colors. One of the things folks began to notice, as I did, was you didn't see folks walking their dog nor did you hear their barks or a cat's meow. It was simple. Most folks, at least in our community, gave their pets up to be given the death pill or they did it themselves and like a lot of folks, they simply buried their pet in their back yard. But you could hear the birds, and it was grand to hear!

June got here and our son graduated from high school and was already signed up for college and, fortunately, we had set aside the monies to send him. The second Friday of June was the day. It seemed like everyone in town was there (not really, though our small town has three high schools)! About five hundred teens were graduating-caps, gowns, speeches, the same thing a thousand other high schools are doing across the country. Naturally we had the video camera. All the in-laws and out-laws were there, and of course, his walk across the stage is short and sweet, but it's taped so it's in the family album!

We had a party for him at the house with several of his friends joining us. Seems like most are heading to one college or another. The party lasted until past 10 P.M.

We spent a couple hours cleaning up and just as I was about to call it a night my son said, "Dad, can we talk for a moment?"

I said, "Sure, son, what is it?"

"You know that Bible you left on the kitchen table? Well, I have been reading it and after almost a month now of research, I have decided to follow your steps and become a Christian. Can you help me out from here?"

I grabbed him and hugged him and, yes, a tear or two fell down my face. All I could think to do was yell out a Hallelujah, but his sister and the Mrs. had already slipped back to bed. What a wonderful thing to happen. I was so excited I wanted to go out in the streets and yell, but I calmed myself down and soon the lights were out and all were asleep.

My daughter was doing well in school. There was only a few days break between ending high school and starting college so my son was already back to classes and homework. The Mrs. was being asked to work overtime and she tells me she is going to have to do so or look for another job!

June left, July got here. The temperatures all over the world began heating up. The heaters were off and the air conditioning started. There were reports that the ice caps on both the North Pole and the South Pole had higher temperatures than ever recorded and if the ice began melting it could cause major, major flooding on lands now occupied by multi-millions of people. Scientists sent up many weather satellites trying to figure out why this was happening and their only conclusion was that the earth's rotation was hanging so that the North and South Poles were not at the positions they have been the last billion plus years. Also the earth had changed in the way it sits and rotates so it could continually change the entire world, as we knew it – i.e. weather patterns-cold, hot, ice, snow, rain, thunder, tornadoes, earthquakes, sand storms, snow on mountaintops, and flooding. All could change if this rotation of the earth turns out to be true.

August and September were extremely hot, but not so bad that one couldn't live in it. It was reported the temperature even in our small community was seven degrees hotter than any time ever recorded by our weather bureau. It made one stop and think about this rotation of the earth theory. My son asked me about how to become an actual Christian. I shared with him what I did. He asked me to witness him do the same so he prayed the prayer I did to the God we both now worship. He baptized himself just like I did and I watched him. He said he had the same feelings I did when he came up out of the water-sooo goood! Then we asked and answered questions about God and the Bible. We didn't know anyone else to go to that we could really trust. As we both agreed, whoever we asked should have vanished and they didn't. Why not?

So we simply worship God the best way we know how and live our life out on a daily basis the best way we know how. And to be honest, life wasn't that bad. We didn't have all the luxuries of living the way we did before the vanishing and the New World Organization, but it was still acceptable!

Speaking of the NWO it's now been nine months since those eight major worldwide laws went into effect along with the death pill. So far this is the result of those laws-the <u>death pill</u> took about a billion people, which has the world population now down to about 5 billion, but with new babies being born and those who die naturally, or by suicide or by accident or by the death pill, according to what I have read, it's about equal between births and deaths on a monthly basis. So far scientists, farmers, horticulturists, weather satellites have been able to keep enough food on the planets to not have anyone die of starvation-so far!

We have been helped by the NWO order on <u>Food Rationing</u>. The food supply seems to be adequate. I have heard that the black market for food coupons is an enormous business! I wouldn't want to get caught doing that. The penalties are severe, from what I've heard. The <u>Utility Rationing</u> is facing the same situation. To those honest, it's not a bad law. We all adjust. To the dishonest, it's an awful penalty if you get caught! The <u>Fuel Rationing</u> has also worked out quite well. We all seem to do the same thing we did before with less fuel than we used before. In fact, I asked the Mrs. just a week ago if she thought we were driving less or shopping less or doing what we wanted to do less. She looked at me with one word, "Huh"!

The <u>Crime Deterrent Law</u> is not working one iota! It seems people just don't care if they live or die. With the death pill situation everyone has started to just not care if they get caught. Go to a Judge with no jury and no appealing. The law so far has not deterred crime. In fact, according to reports, it's worse now than before the Crime Determent Law went into effect!

The <u>One World Language</u> has also not gone over well. It's tough to make people change their country's language to make it secondary and English first. I don't know how the NWO is going to force this into effect.

The <u>Child Bearing</u> Law has been somewhat successful. Either the guy or gal is able to take the pill to not have children. This has been a major help. In fact, if it wasn't for that this world would have billions too many mouths to feed! But it's sad to watch on TV where a couple went and conceived a second child and they had to give up the child right at their birthing room and the childless couple (all done through a Lottery System) was waiting immediately to receive this new baby. It's sad, but it's a reality!

The Everybody Works law has probably been the most successful of the eight (nine if you count the death pill). I guess it only proves humans were not meant to not work. The NWO has demanded that employers, states, countries, cities, municipalities, prisons, everyone join in on this effort and there is hardly an iota of unemployment. The world is working to keep the human race alive and well, so far!

And the last law, the Air Pollution law is trying to work, but even the NWO has had a tough time making the world polluters comply. I can't figure it out. We are having massive weather changes; the satellites prove it's caused by air pollution. You show this to the polluters and they argue it's not them. It's the same old word that's been around since the beginning of time, "GREED." September passes and I have to admit it was the hottest summer I can ever recall.

October is here, November and another Thanksgiving. This time we talked my mom and dad to have it at their home. All showed up. It was joyous (no turkey still!). Mom and my Mrs. did an extremely good job cooking from what's available on store shelves and food rationing. It was almost an all-day event. I got a chance to talk about Christianity to a couple of relatives.

They said they would think about it. It excited me just to discuss the subject! The cold came in just like it left-fast and furious. My son and I did a tremendous amount of sharing about God with one another. My daughter and the Mrs. still were not receptive to this notion. She and my daughter however, have mentioned that they both enjoy the changes they have seen in the two of us since we became Christians.

Christmas arrived and so did the awful cold. Scientists who study weather patterns and those who study the earth's rotation all say it's happening very slowly but it's happening. If the earth changes just an inch or a foot off its axis in a year's time from the way it's been rotating since the beginning, it could be disastrous for all mankind. It will again melt ice and flood lands. It will cause rain to fall where it hasn't, and it will cause heat to be hot when it's supposed to be cold. It's not going to happen overnight but those science guys say it's happening!

We had a wonderful Christmas time. Seems with all that's going on no one wanted to come over. We didn't want to go out. So this year everybody just stayed in. I bought a used, easy-to-read and understand Bible for the Mrs. and my daughter. They were appreciative. It was a time for my son and me to really share what Christmas was and what it was not!

Before that we all agreed to do our traditional thing and that was to again go out and buy a Christmas tree, even in these difficult times. On to our favorite place to buy one, but the pickings were slim at best. I asked the guy in charge why was this so since in years past, about this same time, there were trees galore. He told me, "Too cold, not enough rain, ground not good, nobody is interested in harvesting Christmas trees as no profit in them as most folks have given up on Christmas as a celebrated holiday. It is just no longer a good business to be in!"

I, of course, gasp at all he said and simply asked him, "Where did you gather all this information?"

He answered, "Isn't it a bit colder around here than usual?"

"Yep," I answered.

"Seen it raining a lot around here or any other parts?"

"Nope," I answered.

"Know anybody growing anything anywhere?"

"Nope," I answered.

"Know anybody making any money at an honest business anymore?"

I said, "Yea, me. I am in the computer business. It's honest and profitable."

At than he said, "Lucky!" Then he asked, "Know many folks celebrating anything these days?"

And I responded, "You're right about that. Few if that many."

With that we walked around the tree lot to see if we could find one that was to our liking and soon my daughter yelled out, "Found one."

With that we all dashed over to see her pick! It was nice. It would be ok for us. We paid the gent who gave me his negative report and took our lone tree home. We did as usual and pulled out all the decorations and began piling them on this halfway decent tree. In a short while it was all done.

The four of us went out in front of our house and took pride at what we saw through the bay window. But then my son said, "Dad, have you noticed?"

What, "I asked.

"No one that I can see has a tree in their window as they had in years past!"

At that I looked across the street, peaked at our neighbor's, too! I then took a short walk down the street, even went so far as to go (after the Mrs. and kids went indoors as it was bitterly cold) to my neighbor's house and knock on his door. He answered and I asked, "No Christmas tree?"

At that he simply said just as the guy at the Christmas lot said, "What's there to celebrate?" He closed the door before I could even respond to his question.

Back to the house I headed. Indoors we still all admired our accomplishment. Of course, all wanted to know what our neighbor said and I simply said he said "Bah Humbug," whatever that old saying meant. We did some church, some Internet, some TV, and a bite of canned goodies. Then it was all to bed.

Christmas Eve Day and all awake. No gifts under the tree so about 10:30, after breakfast I headed to town to try to gather up a few things for the family. Not much traffic, but I can understand that at $10.00 per gallon of gas who can afford to drive with an allotment of only one full tank a week it's all computerized so you can't get more no matter who you are least you barter or buy black market. You just couldn't go very far.

Anyway, I made my way to our local mall, parked and went into the shops. For a Christmas Eve I was astonished that not many cars were in the parking lot and few folks were shopping. Surprisingly only a few shops were open (on Christmas Eve)!! But I found an old favorite, went in to browse, found a gift for the Mrs. and one for each of the kids, paid for them and had them wrapped and tagged. Naturally, being the inquisitive guy I am, I asked the gal who waited on me what her opinion was of such low traffic on Christmas Eve.

"Do you know something I don't," she asked me.

"What do you mean?" I responded.

"Who's celebrating, who's interested, who has money, who can afford to drive here, who is doing what you're doing. Look around, see anybody else with a smile like it's Christmas Eve?"

With that I paid the bill, took my three packages, said Merry Christmas anyway, and left. Sadly she was right! You could have dropped a bomb in that mall and no one would have been affected; it was that empty! I drove home naturally despondent over the disgusting truth of what she and my neighbor said.

I put the three (only three) gifts under the tree and spent the rest of the day doing zippo. It was too cold outside! No relatives were coming over nor have we been invited, so only thing on TV is news of worldwide disasters, which seem to occur every hour on the hour! Nighttime got here, the Mrs. fixed us, as always, a great meal out of the minimal foods she has to work with. After dinner I asked if we could all sit before we cleared up our dirty dishes.

All said 'yes' and I simply said, "This is a tough time for all the world. The vanishings, the NWO taking over the world and implementing rules most folks object to, the death pill, no Christmas celebration by the mass majority, yet we, as a family, have tons to celebrate: A. We are healthy. B. None of us are starving. C. We still have our home and car. D. We get our rationings on time. E. We all have learned to adjust. F. You two are in good schools. G. We both have good career incomes. H. Two of us are born-again Christians. I. We don't awake to fears as many do daily. J. We live in a good neighborhood. K. Our town has not been subjected to the brutality that many have faced. L. No one, as yet, in our family has had to take the death pill. We can celebrate Christmas with a smile and joy in our hearts!"

With that said all looked at me seemingly with looks of "Huh, Dad" and got up, cleaned off their plates and all headed to their individual rooms, including my Mrs. I did the last of the cleanup since now that I am home 24/7 it's made me into Mr. Mom.

After all, the kids are in class eight hours a day and spend another two hours plus doing homework and the Mrs. works a minimum 8-hour day and many times 10 and 12 hour days in overtime. I put in, maybe, five hours a day at my computer business here in my house so who should do the taking care of the house and yard. I would be the only logical answer and fortunately for me and them, I like it!

It was late and soon Christmas Eve was over and Christmas morning got here. Sure wasn't like past Christmases. I was first up and had to awake all to meet at the Christmas tree. Apparently all had gotten up during the wee hours and put a gift under the tree besides my three. Soon all showed up and gifts were handed out by the Mrs. There were no big surprises. There were 'thank yous' and hugs! Soon all worked their way into the kitchen for mother's Christmas morning breakfast. That was the real gift! This woman can make seaweed taste great. It took an hour to go through a meal with lots of chitchat like: what's on the next year's horizon, college, another high school graduation by #1 daughter, maybe a hospital promotion, and most certainly an even better year in my computer business. It was refreshing to hear all the plans being made and, there was even some laughter! (Difficult because of the doom and gloom of the world's headaches.)

A week later we all said 'adios' to the year that just passed and hello to the one arriving. Not much of a New Year celebration and could not find one country celebrating on TV. Guess there's too much heartache to celebrate.

January was here and all back to school and work. The news was the same day in and day out. Immorality was rampant, but sadly no one called it that any more. Homosexuality was more pervasive and open than in all the years I have lived. In fact, the mood in their world was "It's ok to be gay!" It was an attack on morality, but the world seemed to come to the conclusion that God had taken his "saints" home and those left, all six billion plus still had to deal with, I guess, the devil (whoever he was or is). What's the use of morality, then, if God isn't interested in what He left on planet earth.

Of course, I most certainly disagreed for I felt God took those who were His. He has the ability to do it again and besides that, His second coming as described in the Bible, had not occurred as yet. So why not be good? Why not be a Christian? Why not believe there is a second chance? Why not, I kept asking myself, why not?

I am back to the grind of working my computer business, which seemed to get busier by the day. With billing, collecting, and even with all being done via the Internet, there were still accounts out there that would use my insight; then not pay for whatever reason. It's a headache but it comes with the territory of being self-employed, independent.

Soon January flew by, the NWO was busy based on all I saw via the TV, the Internet, newspapers; trying to keep order by one governmental body has to be more difficult than two hundred lesser taking care of their own nations. From all one can see, hear, read, it's a mess and the biggest mess is trying to make all nationalities, races, religions, languages, and money into all being equal. You just don't change a thousand year old tradition easily even if one hundred million humans left earth in the blink of an eye! People are still mad, upset, and angry at what is being done, especially in the Muslim world. Trying to get them converted to a belief in a one world government (no matter what God they believed in) is a monstrous job and I am told a few of them were gone, on March 9th over a year ago. That took me for a surprise but then who am I to say anything as I am still here!

February arrived and the only thing changing that I could see was rationing and allotments. To be downright honest, there are still way too many humans for what is left to eat, left to have fuel, left to drink clean water, and left to breath the unclean air. The pill, even though now mandatory, isn't working because although it's been eons since it was put into law, few have volunteered and those it truly effects have found ways to hide from being caught and forced a needle of death. It's not a bright future for earth's inhabitants!

March got here and naturally all were scared to death of March 9th at 3 P.M. for now it's the second anniversary and all the world, even though it's a worldwide day of remembrance, feel something terrible is going to again happen!

Chapter Eight

"TWO YEARS HAVE PASSED"

CHAPTER EIGHT
"Two Years Have Passed"

It got here. It was a cold, windy day. No rain but it looks like a rainy day and even smells like rain. Usually it's a day off for the world again, for the second year, to remember all those multi-millions who left planet earth with no goodbyes, no farewells, no last hug, no last kiss, no last wave. For multitudes it was still twenty-four months later, a day to mourn. The Mrs. had to work today. It's double time, but since we don't really need the extra money we all wished she could have been here with us. Suicides are up a thousand percent. Babies are being born faster than ever! With the death pill or vaccination, the accidents, and all the illnesses that plague the world, there is simply no rest for those in her profession. As she left this dreadful morning I gave her a hug and kiss and told her to care for herself as well as all the others who need her. With that, she was off to the hospital, thankfully not very far from where we live.

Soon the kids woke up. Our daughter, who is learning to be the cook her mother is, fixed us two men a wonderful quick breakfast. By 9 A.M. all were dressed. It feels strange to have the kids off on a Wednesday. "So what's on the schedule today Dad as we both have no plans, no homework, zippo to do?"

"Well guys, I am as bad off as you. I haven't any plans, especially with your mom not here to enjoy whatever the day brings," I responded.

With that my daughter went to make all the unmade beds; my son went outdoors in the cold to take a short walk, and I turned on the TV to see what the world had to say for itself at 10 A.M. on a day of remembrance. It wasn't good! It seems crime is up ten thousand percent even with people knowing that the world government won't put up with it and punishment is severe. The mindset is, "Who cares!" So thieves, rapists, murderers, thugs, terrorists, and the like continue their rampage in every corner of earth.

Fortunately for us, our community has not been hit with such horrors as one can see daily on TV. I guess many think God has left planet earth and removed His spirit so what's left but to kill and plunder and, of course, I don't agree with that thinking one iota. If God is not here how did my son and I become a Christian? Why did we baptize ourselves? Why were we able to find a Bible and have the ability to read it with faith? How is it, good still roams the earth searching to overcome evil? No I believe God is still here and is alive and well. The church doors are all open today as one could see on TV. The Jews are attending theirs, the Christians theirs, the Catholics theirs, the Muslims theirs and yes, the Atheists are still as active as ever. God knows there will always be unbelievers so nothing has changed in their world.

It's noon and all have joined me in our family room watching the TV as if it were back in the old days when the family sat around watching the New Year's Eve celebration worldwide. We had a snack or lunch. Both kids decided to go read or scan the Internet, but I continued my sofa sitting watching the news unfold until that moment of 3 P.M. Naturally the whole world was doing as I was, wondering if another catastrophic incident would happen. But by 3:10 P.M. zero happened but lots of folks including little old me had a lump in our throats and that includes the government top to bottom. By 3:30 all was back to a normal day. The worry was over for another 365 days. At least that's the hope.

The Mrs. got home a little early as those who have been working a lot of overtime as she had got a break. "How was it at work, Sweetie?" I asked as she came through the door.

"Hectic, monstrous, overworked, not enough staff and too many tales of sorrow to even begin and yet it was a normal day in the times we are living," she responded. She took off her jacket.

I made her a cup of her favorite tea and asked her where she would like to sit. She responded, "In front of the TV as I want to hear what went on at 3 P.M. when I was trying to save a woman who was attempting suicide by swallowing a bunch of lethal pills."

So she grabbed the tea and the two of us plopped ourselves on our favorite sofa and turned on news, which is 99.99% of what's on every channel these days. It seems to outsell the old sitcoms and movie channels so this is what the world watches, daily 24/7 to see what's next.

It was about 5 P.M. when breaking news hit while I was in the kitchen tidying up. It seems a band of criminals are trying to overtake the ruling party headquartered at the old United Nations Building in New York City. They have surrounded the building and are demanding a new government! It didn't last long. Within less than an hour a massive amount of Special Forces showed up and from a short distance a sharpshooter simply killed each one, even with them holding hostages. It was real life drama right on our television set.

By 7 P.M. just a mere two hours later not one was alive. The crowd had dispersed and one would have never known the event happened lest you actually saw it firsthand. The night wore on. The Mrs. was exhausted, the kids had school tomorrow and I had a full day planned in my business so by 10:00 it was lights out all through the house and off to sleep after another tragic day.

The next morning it was still bitter cold from a northeast wind that just froze all it touched. The Mrs. grabbed a quick bite, the kids as well, and soon I was left with another day alone so decided to put my business on hold for a few hours and again take a drive around to see what's happened and yes, gas still at $10.00 a gallon and only one tank per week per car doesn't allow much. I needed to see what was going on in this community that I have lived in for too many years to recall. Got in a quick shower and dressed, grabbed my keys and out the door I went.

My first goal was to check out the racquetball club. As I drove up I again noticed few cars in the parking lot unlike the old days when one couldn't find a place to park at this time of day. On into the club and it was dead so being inquisitive I asked the front desk folk what was going on, "Sir, no one is here because, to put it up front, no one can afford the gas to get here, and no one wants to use their allotment of gas to get here. Everybody is afraid of everybody. No one has an interest in exercise. I am sure the new owners will be sorry they bought this business even though they bought it for $.10 on the dollar at an auction. I hope that tells you why you see what you see!"

With that I simply said, "Thanks," and walked through this once vibrant place! No one playing racquetball, no one exercising, no basketball players, so on into the men's locker room just to see if all was the same and it was. One guy was in the steam room and another taking a shower. With that I made my way back out, despondent over what I had learned.

I drove over to the ritzy area where the family that owned this club lived. Learned his family all vanished leaving a gorgeous 5,000 square foot home now empty as a barn house. To my utter surprise it wasn't what it was. Lawns were not moved, grass turned ugly because no one cared, and a multitude of houses empty including his since no one either had the money nor desire to live in the land of the once wealthy. It was sad looking at row upon row of multimillion dollar homes as vacant as an empty parking lot. I have to believe folks finally figured out that you can't buy your way into heaven so why live as if you could down here. (My assumption, of course.)

With seeing those two disasters I worked my way back to our local grocery store to buy some needed food for the family. I parked and went on in. It was not busy, to say the least, and the shelves were slim pickings. No meat market as there's none to sell, vegetable and fruits empty except for some not so good-looking potatoes. About the only thing that was readily available were canned goods. So I loaded up the cart with what I thought we needed along with some paper products. Checked through and, of course, found no one in a smiling mood. Just downright frowns is all I could see. At home, park and unload car. On into the house to find all as I had left it.

Turn on TV to see if any updated news and was hit with a biggie. The government has decided because of so much fraud, identity theft, computer theft, stealing purses and wallets, breaking business's windows to grab cash, that in the next 60 days the entire world is going to a cashless, credit less world!! The proposal is to live via a fingerprint, an eye recognition, or a DNA recognition. That is what is on the table. All sounds ridiculous. How is one to buy and sell without cash or credit card? Think, too, of the onslaught of those businesses which ripped off the world for loans with 30%, 40%, 50% interest rates! After that thought, this new idea might not be so bad.

Spent rest of day going through all my messages, nothing urgent so worked until kids home at 4:30 and Mrs. walked in at 5:00. She fixed us dinner, thanked me for grocery shopping and for putting away everything in its rightful place. Told them about driving to the racquetball club and ritzy home area. They all just kind of looked at me as if to say, "Dad, what did you expect to see in these times we are going through?"

It was another day. I shared the government's idea on a cashless world and my son's comment was, "About time!"

The night wore on. All did what we all normally do on a work/school night. Soon it was a goodnight, lights out and before we knew it we were all asleep.

March flew by and so did April. May, June, and July got here and the cold turned to heat. With the cost of utilities it was almost impossible to run the air conditioner too long. Fact is I don't know how the folks can make it no matter how much money they have. Auto gas, insurance, food, utilities, mortgage payment, school, clothing, medical cost and forget retirement as it's all but gone. The Mrs.'s 401K at the hospital was shut down due to a variety of things- poor investments, management theft, brokers' exorbitant fees and so on. Living in these times, even in the good, old safe USA is not easy and pity you if you're trying to get on welfare as it was shut down two years ago! The cost of living is astronomical even for the upper class and no matter who one is, all have an allotment. Even if you have big bucks, it doesn't do any good!

I decided to call my old buddy who wanted $100,000 to invest with him in the auction business to ask him his thought on this new government's idea to be enacted in 60 days to stop identity theft. He always seems to have some insight as to what's on the horizon. "Hey old buddy what's up? How is the auction business and before you tell me, what's your thoughts on this new worldwide law about I.D. theft. I am all ears on your words of wisdom."

"Well, old friend, first you should have gone in with me as I have quadrupled my investment. It's time consuming and a bit eerie at times, mostly because the heirs to these homes and businesses fight you all the way through the court system to get what they feel is legally theirs. I have dealt with many who are so disturbed that a relative vanished and not them. They are simply stupefied that they can't come to grips with the fact they are still here. Then reality sets in and now they want the most money they can get and it's been extremely tough. Remember that racquetball king where he and his Mrs. and two kids all vanished? Well, I got to buy his business and his monstrous house for about $.50 on the dollar and I was the highest bid. Luckily I sold it for about $.65 on the dollar and made a good deal of money from just those two sales.

"That's one you and I could have shared as I know you're a racquetball player at that club. Anyway your question on the I.D. theft. First of all we know the old Social Security card, the green card, the passport, all have to go in the world we live in. Why does one need a passport if one government is running the whole nine yards? They have suggested several alternatives, but the only one that will work is the fingerprint, unless a guy has no hand! Then a toe print will have to do. I just don't see the eye thing as too many folks are blind. The DNA thing would be too difficult to manage. They even have one where all will have to have a microchip put under the skin but fear came because folks could kill others to get their chip. I think you're going to find the idea of a fingerprint the most logical. It's easy to invent a machine that sits on a counter in every situation. Put your thumb on it, it reads it and whatever monies you have in your bank account are subtracted with your purchase. You get a receipt for your purchase and out the door you go!"

At that I said, "You're right" and "I am still not sorry I did not go into the auction business with you. Who needs those nightmares? You're right with the fingerprint and one last thing before I hang up."

"Yea, what is it," he responds.

"Have you given any thought to becoming a Christian?"

Then out of his mouth he gasps, "What, those were the ones that vanished. Don't you think it's a bit late? That's like closing the barn door after the horse got out. No. Not impressed and don't think you're going to have much luck pushing that agenda besides that, how is your new computer business?"

At that I said, "Good," and said my thanks for his input and would talk with him later.

It was much too warm in the house so I cranked on the air conditioner and the air felt so good. I still had a bunch of work to do and no way could I do it in that heat no matter what the cost. Soon I heard a knock on the door and it was my neighbor.

"Hi, old friend," I said to him. "What brings you to my abode?"

He then said sternly, "Don't you realize the cost of electricity with an air conditioner? You're the only one with it turned on as far as I know. Best if you just jump in a shower or carry around a cold wet towel. Anyway, I just wanted to make sure you're OK."

I then smiled and replied, "Yep, all is well and I think I can afford it even if it's a bit expensive but thanks for thinking of me."

With that he turned and went back to his 90+ degree heat in his house. I got into my work and did what had to be done and before I knew it the kids and Mrs. were marching in the door. Of course, all said, almost in unison, "Air conditioning!"

"Yep, was too hot and I am not going to work in heat!"

The Mrs. said, "Thank you, I work in a hospital where air conditioning is mandatory, yet even there the temp is set at 80° so it isn't by any means cool."

Nothing more was said. Dinner was prepared. I shared the

identity idea and they all agreed finger printing would be the easiest form of I.D. The night flew by. At 10:00 turned off air and all headed to bed for, yes, a warm night's rest.

Not much happened next couple of months. But by the end of September now two and a half years after the vanishing the government said that by year's end all forms of I.D., all forms of monies (paper or coin), all forms of signing legal papers, everything would be eliminated and finger printing only would take effect 01-01-next year. Of course, all the world wondered how it would be enacted, but the government did its homework. They had a small simple unit created. It's tied to all the banks, the banks are tied to the government and so it seemingly will work but who knows until it's actually put in place. If you wanted to turn your cash into credit, you could go to the local bank and ask that the cash be credited to your account. It must be done by the year's end. No more check writing, no more credit cards, and no numbers to deal with. All bills got paid electronically through one's bank account using your fingerprint. The bank then forwarded it on to the government and "Big Brother," as it was called in my younger days, was here at last!

October and November got here and I again convinced the Mrs. to allow me to invite the family to come to our home for this event. Thanksgiving came and lo and behold, my parents (in their early seventies, thank God), her parents (same ages as mine), and a couple siblings came and by 3 P.M. on Thanksgiving Day we had twelve people in our home. Wow, that was a treat! I said a prayer of thanks. We sat down to a dinner that we are all used to by now, no turkey just simple canned foods. The Mrs. knows how to make something out of nothing so we all thanked her.

After dinner my pop asked if he could have a private talk with me and I said, "Absolutely."

We stepped into the living room where no one else was and he said, "Son, I have heard you have become a Christian, and not to be hard on you, but why? Aren't you and all those that have done so just a tad bit late in your decision? I also want to apologize for not being a church goer all those years you and your siblings were growing up. No excuse, just never saw the need for it. We had all the things one wanted so I simply assumed that was enough. Major mistake, but it's water under the bridge. What good is it now?"

At that I said, "Pop, let's sit" and we sat on the couch, "Dad, just because we blew it the first time what's to say God won't do this again. He has not returned in the skies as said in His Holy Bible. Why not believe that it can happen again and what harm is there in believing?"

At that Pop said, "Son, apparently you haven't heard."

"Heard what," I responded.

"It's rumored worldwide that this crisis set upon humankind is the fault of the Christian religion. It's been again rumored that soon it will be outlawed to claim one is a Christian.

At that I said, "Yep, a rumor."

With that we both got up and soon all were saying their goodbyes, thank yous, and we all said we have to do this again soon. And by 7:00 P.M., it was all quiet.

We as a family all jumped in to clean up, dishes, cups, towels, and napkins. Before long it was done and we all took a long sigh of relief and almost in unison said, "Do we want to do that again? What a job feeding and caring for family, but, yes, it was worth the effort."

Finally all found a seat in the family room and before the TV went on I told them what my dad said was a rumor. With that they all sloughed it off and said, "Dad, there are a thousand rumors a day in the world we live in. Are we as a family going to believe or not believe?"

Soon night had fallen, bed was looking good and by 10:30 it was time to say my good nights.

Winter came with the winds blowing, rain falling, hail hitting and some flooding, though not enough to harm property or lives. Christmas was upon us. Honestly, I just thought we celebrated – remembering the scraggly tree and the few decorations. My son then made the comment, "Pop, anyone can see that no neighbors are doing what we still are doing! I'm wondering if we should even be doing this yet, what is Christmas without a tree with decorations showing itself at our bay window? We are, as you know, the only ones for blocks that are 'celebrating.'"

No response from anyone. On Christmas morning there was one gift for each of us as the places to shop are far fewer in number this year than last. A nice day, sun was out, but it was cold so had the heater on and fireplace going both at same time. The Mrs. fixed a nice dinner and late that Christmas night it was on to 'na na' land. Soon we again said adios to last year and said hello to the new year, which arrived on time never missing a second and before we knew it we were all back at the grind with both kids now in college. The expense of keeping them there is a bit higher than we budgeted, but we survived another year and will get through this one as well.

Chapter Nine

"THREE YEARS HAVE PASSED"

CHAPTER NINE
"Three Years Have Passed"

It is March 9th and our world's third anniversary was just about to become another reality. We had been attending a small church about a mile away from home, but the attendance is small compared to what I have been told it was prior to the vanishing, but who can blame most folks. Even my Mrs. and daughter won't go because Christians as they, like the multitudes, simply think it's of no use so why bother. What's done is done, yet my son and I are of a different view as we have come to believe God is big enough to redo what He has done before. Why not I continue to ask myself.

Naturally as the day of mourning gets closer the world gets a bit more nervous thinking some massive catastrophe is going to befall earth. The day got here. The world shuts down all commerce and government to a trickle, and, as in previous years, billions sit in front of their television sets ready to hear what the world's power has to say to us humans. It got to be 3 P.M. and as thought by most nothing would happen, but the CEO/Prime Minister, President, Chief Honchos came on at 3:10 P.M. and said it had a major announcement and would like all to hear it.

Our television sets have a button on it that can re-tape anything you see on television so all you have to do is hit the recall button. It asks you the name of the show and you can ask to see a list a mile long or type in via the remote control the name, the date you saw it, and the time you saw it. If you don't remember those two things, it has several options to help find what you're looking for. Once located you hit play and that program, be it yesterday or last year, will replay on one's television. As we listen to the world's leaders speak I was awestruck at what they said so I replayed it and replayed it and then went to write it down for all to see. I am in shock over their statements the 9th of March beginning at roughly 3:10 P.M.

"As the leaders of the world, whose population is now about 7 billion people, it's imperative we take action to stop the upcoming starvation that will befall humanity lest we do something drastic in the next six months. Let us share with you what has taken place worldwide since the vanishings hit us thirty-six months ago today. Please do not turn off your television set for some mediocre occurrence. What I have to say comes from all ten of us who sit at a table daily discussing what is best for humanity. We have thousands of advisors from every sector of this world so our decision which we are going to share with you today comes from the minds of the best of the best! As you well recall, when we first took over all the world's governments, making it a one-world government we instituted eight rules. These, we were going to enforce in order to survive the future of humanity. Let me review this with you if I may. Here are 13 subjects I am to discuss:

1) We established a one-world government because the fighting in wars was more than the world could handle. When all leaders of all 200 countries showed up to form one government it was by unanimous decision to do so. No one power grabbed control, all is equal in our giving to each country. No one gets more food, fuel, utilities, or luxuries. No one has more poverty or more power than another. This one thing alone has brought stability to a world ready to alienate itself in way too many ways!

2) We brought all the military under one roof giving the world government the ability to stop wars and terrorism which was affecting every corner of earth. Simply put, this has worked most effectively for anyone can see that not one war has erupted since the vanishing and terrorism has come to a screeching halt.

3) We took over all the world's utilities, doling out equally to each country an allotted amount depending on its population. Again this has turned out to be a good thing as

no one has frozen to death or burned up for all is given in equal allotments.

4) We took over all the food distribution again equally sharing what's available by population allotments. This has worked out to the advantage of humanity. The greatest drawback in this scenario is that there simply isn't enough food to feed 7 billion mouths once a day, let alone twice. With all the soil on earth unable to grow anything edible, and the animal population dead or the living ones unable to reproduce, that brought catastrophic problems to our table of decision making.

5) In addition, we took over all gas and oil fields on the entire planet and distribute what's available on a population allotment. Yes, many, if not most of you, can't take a vacation, a Sunday drive, a run to the store for whatever, but know we, as a world government are doing our best to provide you with what's available. One can expect no more from us than our best.

6) We have tried and tried in innumerable ways, to institute a one world language, but it has been of no use thus far. As of today we are giving up on the effort and will allow all countries to speak their own language without being forced to learn another. Perhaps this will bring a bit more peace.

7) We instituted one monetary system but like language this has failed as well. To cut the exorbitant cost of printing money be it a coin or paper, we are instituting a fingerprint system that will go into effect on September 9th this year. Simply put, if you have any cash, you must, in order to be credited to your bank account, return it to your bank to be put back in the treasury to be destroyed. We will, in six months, be a non-cash world and all who wish to buy or sell will do it through a transaction of your fingerprint or a machine. This will hook up to a bank who will then authorize a draft from your account to the one from whom

you are making a purchase. No other means of buying or selling, lest it be bartering, will be allowed. This will put a stop to counterfeiters, thieves, money launderers, scam artists and so on. The once known credit card industry will fold. No more high interest rates because, from September 9th of this year, we will all learn to live on what we have, not on wishful thinking.

8) The birth control system somewhat worked. We, the government, thought that after this long, there would be less mouths to feed but we find now that there are more. This is a problem. We are still in the adjustment stages and will keep you informed of our progress.

9) The death pill, for those in certain categories, has again not gone over as we had expected. We had hoped for a billion less population by this time, but it has in no way done that! We tried voluntary methods and it didn't work. We tried mandatory and that didn't work. The only success we had in this has been the pet elimination. Many a mouth would have starved worldwide but the food saved by not feeding pets went to feed humans. So it's a decree today, on September 9th of this year that all who have to buy or sell will have to use a fingerprint machine. This will tell us who it is, their age, their address, their phone number, and their work ability. If they are found in the worldwide computer to be of 75 years of age, unable to work, or if one is blind, handicapped, or is unable to do their share of work, will be forced to take the pill or be vaccinated. This will eliminate them from the human work force and the need to feed an unproductive mouth.

10) Crime is still a horrible problem. It seems no matter where one lives or works, crime in some way effects our lives. We have tried prison and the death penalty. We have no jury trials and no system to arbitrate. Simply put, if a person is caught during a crime or is known to have committed

a crime they are immediately incarcerated, tried by an appointed judge, sentenced to whatever the judge says. We thought for sure this would put an end to crime. We were mistaken, "major time," so we are increasing our diligence. Soon we will have appointed and trained vigilante groups in all areas in all the world to protect citizens, businesses, and property. They will punish on site, if necessary, but presently they will be trained to know right from wrong and good from evil. They will be allotted according to population and they should be in place by September 9th, this year.

11) The everybody-work plan has probably been our best effort. We have seen men, boys (out of school, of course), women and young girls (also out of school) who have taken up where prisoners used to work, doing a myriad of jobs too countless to mention here. They have been paid a fair wage, not over worked, not enslaved, and from all reports worldwide, it has proven to be the most effective thing we have put in place since the enactment of a one world government, three years ago.

12) Air pollutants have also been a success story, but not the size of the one just discussed. We have cut back considerably on auto traffic simply because all get an allotted amount of gas. Once you have used up that allotment you learn to walk and that alone has cut the air pollutants considerably. Factory pollutants have as well been cut back, but not as much as we'd like to see. That's a goal we are working on. Of course, there are no more animal pollutants because there are virtually none left worldwide.

13) Last of all I need to discuss with you a situation which will be difficult to talk about but it's a must and I have been elected to say this. Ever since the vanishings, folks of all walks of life including me have asked why them and not me. Where did they go, why only a hundred million (estimated), which is less than 1% of our entire world's population? Who

did this and for what reason? Why all the after effects? The land is poisoned, it seems, and unable to grow food of any kind, fruit bearing trees dead with no life in them, all the edible animals dead for no obvious reasons, waterways filled with dead fish, poisoned, and yet pet animals left alive to have to feed.

The only asset the earth had left was the oceans as they have not been touched by this plague if I may call it that. Then there were the after effects of dealing with the millions upon millions of these vanished folks, including things like materialism, houses, businesses, cars, bank accounts, and a multitude too long to list. This began a new breed of folks having to start up a new business. In auctioning off the above items, there could be a new business, a new homeowner, a new car owner, but I have to confess it's still an ongoing business. We have hardly put a dent in dealing with one hundred million vanished peoples' belongings. It's overwhelming to say the least.

Now to the tough part. "Christianity." We have called in the best of the minds worldwide from every corner of earth and have tried to understand, comprehend, take in, why the vanishing and why the disastrous aftermath. After all who in their right mind would take a few and leave the rest to starve to death? So after much debate, much thought, much going over and over, it's been decided to "wipe Christianity off the earth!" I know many of you are gasping and some of you are saying it's about time, so no matter what we do all are not going to be happy. Here is the plan, which will be completed within the next six months. That will be September 9th of this year:

    a.   Close, shut down, tear down, destroy, change to another type of non-Christian church or a business of some sort! Every Catholic/Protestant/Mormon/

any Christian Church worldwide from city to country will all be affected no matter what! None will be spared. All must be destroyed or converted to non-Christian.

b. All material regarding Christianity must and will be destroyed by fire! Bibles, 8-tracks, videos, CD's, books, and movies, will be destroyed by September 9th of this year. If not, a punishment will be laid upon those who resist.

c. All television, radio, Internet stations will go off the air and their material will be destroyed or, if non-Christian, auctioned.

d. All those claiming to be a Christian will have to sign a written prepared statement saying they <u>renounce</u> their belief on or before September 9th of this year. This <u>will be executed via our government agency</u>. This act should not have a long list of non-compliers for I don't see many folks giving up for a course that is past its time!

Now the good news in this last of the list of 13 items is that one can still be a Muslim, a Jew, or an Atheist, as there is no crime in this. It's the Christian religion that has made earth a living mess, and we plan to stamp it out.

Thank you for your patient ear. Thank you for complying with all we have said, but do remember this September 9th these will take effect, no matter what!

1) A fingerprint will be the only way one can do business of any type and all the world must comply.

2) The death pill or vaccination will be mandatory for those it applies to.

3) Vigilante groups per the governments' instructions will be placed in every corner of the earth to stop this crime epidemic.

4) Christianity will cease to be in buildings, or in literature. Believers must comply with the renouncing of their belief.

Again my thanks to you for all the time you have allowed us into your homes and businesses. We wish you the best in these days ahead and we are in hopes you will work with us to make earth a once again livable place.

I sat there with my Mrs. and two kids and could say nothing. It was simply too much to take in. The Mrs. got up from the couch as it now was dinnertime and without a word from anyone she simply went in and prepared a meal for the four of us. As we sat round the table I finally said, "So what's all your thoughts?"

Instantly, all said, "Bah Humbug."

Then my son said, "Dad, if we believe what he just said we might as well hang ourselves now. What a negative guy! To think he is top gun of the world is awful. Wow!"

My daughter then says, "Dad, don't worry, no one will ever find out you're a Christian, nor this brother of mine. So relax!"

At that my Mrs. speaks up and says, "Not so fast with those words. How many folks have you told you're a Christian? Aren't you registered as a member at that church you take us to each Sunday? No, I think it's well known your dad and brother are Christians, but I, as well, don't think they will go through with the threat. Look at the death pill as an example. That hasn't taken off as they said it would!"

I didn't say a word as I needed to take in all that I heard on TV and their comments before I respond to all three with my thoughts. Dinner got over with. Nighttime rolled in. Soon all were off to bed as all, including me, have a busy day ahead and tomorrow starts early. Lights were out and off to a night's sleep. As always, the night goes by quicker than expected and soon the alarms are going off at 6 A.M.

Before one can know what's happening, the kids are off to school and the Mrs. is off to the hospital. I got in a quick shower and dressed and was down to my makeshift office in part of the family room since all I really need is my computer, a desk, chair, a small two drawer file cabinet and I am in business. This morning I thought I would call my old buddy in the auction business to get his thoughts on last night's lengthy talk.

"Hey old friend, how is it these days?" I asked.

"Hey old buddy, great. Business is as good as it can get. The fact is that there isn't enough of me to get done all that has to be done."

I respond. "What do you mean? I thought you had it all under control last time we chatted?"

"Yep, thought so too! The forms however, that you have to fill out for the government on each auction is mind boggling and then maybe I didn't tell you but each piece of property I sell I have to give 25% of whatever I make to the heirs of the property, if I can find them. The government won't allow me to touch the 25% until a one year finding time has passed and if you don't think it's tough tracking down heirs, you haven't seen leg work," he responded.

"Wow, I think that is so neat and so government responsible. I am truly impressed with what you just shared with me. Thank you," I responded.

"So what's up with you? Oh, you're not calling about that comment last night from the head honcho about Christianity, are you?" He asked of me.

"Yea, I kind of wanted to get your feel on it," I responded.

"Ok, here are my thoughts. He is right on. If it weren't for Christianity this world would have kept right on trekking along as it has been for thousands of years. I mean, was your life miserable before the vanishings? No and mine was alright as well, so yes, the world has been turned upside down. Think about issues like food, utilities, and allotments. Now we have fingerprinting, we've lost pets, and there is no meat to eat except canned goods. I mean, you have to admit, we are as a planet a whole lot worse off by far than we were just three years back. I am sure you agree, right?"

"Yes, you're right but let's not forget that vanishing was predicted 2000+ years ago so it had to happen sometime and it just happened to occur during our lives. Won't you agree to that?" I asked of him.

"Yes, I agree but no one expected the after effects. I mean the ground poisoned, all the edible animals found dead in their tracks and no reproduction and trees that bear no fruit. How does this God you admire so much expect seven billion plus to survive? Please tell me and the world if you have an answer to that?" He asked.

"I don't have one, I can't even come up with a fairy tale let alone know God's plan but I do know this. God is not through with us yet because His prediction of His second coming has not occurred as yet!" I responded back.

"Big deal, what do you do in the meantime. All starve waiting for Him to show up. If and when He does, what then? If I were you I would put this Christian thing behind me before you end up standing in front of a firing squad!" He said.

With that we both said adios, talk to you later. I could see he and I were miles apart in our thinking. I got back to my business and worked on it until mid-afternoon. I was tired, so laid on the couch and took a stress nap hoping all I heard in last 24 hours was a pipe dream and I would awake to reality.

As soon as I was asleep the kids came through the door and, of course, we all waited for mom who was late. I called down to the hospital to see what's up. "She left here an hour ago," was the response I got.

I called her on her cell phone and all I got was a recording, so the kids and I jumped in my car to see if we could locate her. About six blocks away there were police cars, an ambulance, and of course, rubberneckers all around. I spotted her car and it was a wreck. I thought for sure she was OK, probably just a fender bender. Out of the car I ran over to the nearest police officer and asked, "This is my wife's car. Where can I find her?"

At that he said, "I am sorry sir, but the lady in that car was dead when she hit this pole and banged her head hard. It killed her instantly!"

I said "No way. That's my wife, maybe she is just hurt."

I ran over to the ambulance where the attendant said, "Want to see if she is your Mrs.?"

"Yes, please." With that he took the sheet off her face. It was her all right, blood and all. At that I asked, "Did you try to save her?"

He responded, "She was dead when we got here."

With tears pouring out of my eyes I went back to the police officer and asked, "What in the world happened do you think?"

"Well, from what I can gather she saw something jump out at her. She swerved the car and at probably 35 mph she hit that pole. That's my guess." I was dumbstruck.

By now the kids had found out and were crying their eyes out as well. Soon the crowd dispersed. The cops left. The ambulance headed to the coroner and we were left standing there numb at the impact of her death. Soon we headed back home. No one could speak, not a peep from all three of us. Total silence! Off to bed we all went, the kids to theirs and me to mine alone for the first time in 25 years plus of marriage. As I lay there all I could do was ask why over and over again, why and why with not even a slight of an answer.

I was so sick to my stomach I went in and threw up whatever I had in me. I went out to the kitchen and sat bewildered and slowly made a list of who to call now before they heard it on the news:

The hospital
Her parents
Her siblings
My parents
My siblings
Her closest friend

That took an hour plus but I had to do it. With that I crawled back in bed hoping what had just happened was a nightmare and nothing more! Soon, at 4 A.M., I was awake and on my knees asking God why this took place, why her not being Christian versus me, being one? Surely that in my mind would have made more sense. After some more tears and wishing, I headed to the kitchen. Had some canned O.J. and just sat there. Before I knew it the kids were dressed and with a kiss on the forehead by my daughter it was off to school as they both said it would be the best medicine for them. It would allow me to deal with what faced us. Of all that's going on in the world one would think that even a death of a spouse would not take priority but for me it did. It was overwhelming.

At 8:30 I got a call from the coroners to stop by to again identify my wife as actually my wife and the hospital called asking if I could make my way in to get her things out of her locker and her last paycheck. So, into a quick shower. The hospital first and, of course, all were sympathetic. I cleaned out what little she had in her small locker, picked up her paycheck at payroll, then over to the coroner to again go through the horrible job of identifying her, which I reluctantly did.

At the house, I found my parents and hers waiting at my front door. All came in and all sobbed uncontrollably. Then, of course, I had to answer all their questions-what happened exactly, was she in any pain, when is the funeral, have you chosen a burial plot, what are we three going to do without her, etc., etc., etc. By 1 P.M. they all four left, broken hearted as I was. I laid on the couch until the kids got home and I told them of today's events. No one was hungry so we just kind of sat with few words spoken. Bedtime got here and all headed to a night's rest.

The next day I awoke to find them already gone to school. I was up and took a quick shower and dress. I decided to put work aside and plan for her final arrangements-

A) Funeral home
B) Pick out a casket
C) Sign form to have her transferred
D) Burial plot at local cemetery
E) Day set for all to happen

That took the better part of a full day and again when kids got home shared what I had done and they both agreed it was best I did it alone rather than them traipsing along as it would have been just too painful. A weekend passed and on Monday we had the funeral. I had put it in our local paper and on the Internet so lots of folks showed up. I had the pastor from the church I attended do the services. We drove out to the gravesite, and had her buried. All dropped a flower on top of her casket as it was being lowered and within no time the area was empty of people, only the kids and myself stayed behind. A friend had driven my car out so we could drive back home.

I shared with my two kids how I felt about my decision to become a Christian and how I was not about to change that regardless of the outcome. At that my son spoke up and said, "Dad, I became a Christian because of you and your deep faith, but I am not ready to die for this belief as I know you are. So will you, can you, forgive me if I sign those papers the government is pushing on the campus to renounce one's Christian belief. Can you please say 'yes,' Dad?"

At that I could say nothing but, "Son, you are an adult so you have to decide if that's what you wish to do. Then you have my OK." With that we got up, watched the gravediggers come over and move things around and begin to shovel dirt onto my loving wife's casket. We said goodbye to her and headed to the car. It had been an extremely emotional day so words were kept to a minimum.

Chapter Ten

"THE FINALITY"

CHAPTER TEN
"The Finality"

Time moved on swiftly. Soon spring was here, flowers were blooming, a few smiles from the general public could be seen on folks' faces. It got to be July now with only August and September before those four items supposedly will start:

1) Fingerprinting
2) Death Pill
3) Vigilante groups
4) Christianity

The world seemed, via the television and Internet, to be in a better mood somehow. By this time I had gathered all the Mrs.' insurance papers together, had filed a claim, and at this time have already received a good sized check for her couple of life insurance policies and have deposited it in our bank account. One of the things I was upset about was the hospital's view on "worldwide free medical care." They were against it as was my Mrs., but when I went in to pick up some papers on her behalf, I was locked into an unseemly argument with one of the top day hospital personnel. Why he chose me to argue with is far beyond my understanding. He felt the old system of buyer beware was far greater than simply giving free medical service to any and all who asked.

Of course, my only question to him was, "Who could afford the cost to continue buying insurance. No one I know of! I have to assume you're upset as it has hit your own pocketbook!"

With that he turned and walked away. I ask though, who can argue against free medical care worldwide with no premiums to pay, no claims to fill out, no card to carry, able to use any doctor, hospital, pharmacy. What's wrong with that? In addition, no matter where we travel, work, reside, one is covered! This applies to all forms of medical care, be it a medical doctor or dentist or any other!

July slipped by. 'The kids are doing great in school. I have learned how to not only be a housekeeper, but how to cook with canned foods. August got here and one day midweek I got a knock at my door. It was two gents who introduced themselves as government employees assigned to get Christians to sign affidavits disavowing their belief in Christianity. I invited them both in and the three of us sat on the couch across from one another.

"How successful have you been thus far in getting Christians to sign such a form?"

"Quite good. Fact is I can only think of two individuals who refused and they did sign such a form stating they refuse to compromise their Christian belief!"

"Wow, out of how many have you asked?" I inquired.

"About 300 I would say so far," they said.

"300 and only two said no?" I asked with shock.

"Yep," was their response.

"Well, now you can add three to your list. Where is the form to sign saying I won't give up my Christian belief?" I asked.

"Are you sure you're willing to face a firing squad on September 9, this year if you sign this?" They asked.

I responded, "Yep."

"Wow," they looked at each other and said to themselves, "That's religion in reality! Fine, sign here and someone will be in touch." With that they got up and left leaving me their card in case I changed my mind, even at the last moment.

I closed the door and said to myself, "Now look what you have gone and done!" But I was feeling great about my decision.

The kids got home and I decided to not say anything at this time. A few days passed and my son happened to see those guys' business card on a table and asked me, "Dad these are the same two guys who roamed the campus trying to get all to sign that form, saying one renounces their Christianity."

"Well, did you sign it," I asked.

"Of course not and you knew I wouldn't, didn't you?"

At that I went over and gave him a bear hug and said, "Are you sure?"

He responded, "Yep."

My daughter happened to pop in and said, "What's all the discussion about?"

At that he said to his sister, "Just man talk!"

I fixed us a quick dinner. We watched a bit of TV and they headed up for homework and another day had passed. August flew by and September 1st got here.

I got a phone call from my old auction buddy, "Ready to die for your belief?" He asked.

"What do you mean by that?" I asked.

"It's on TV, all those who signed a form saying they would not renounce their Christianity will be executed by the Vigilante Group on September 9th, nine days from today, so I am assuming you're not going through with this silliness."

At that I said to him, "Not only am I willing to die for such a cause, but my son is as well!"

At that all he could do was start to cry on the phone. "Do you know you're only a few who have decided on this nonsense? What's going to happen to your daughter, your business, your home, your bank accounts, your parents and siblings, your friends like me? Have you given any thought to their missing you and your son?"

I responded, "Yes, I have given all that thought, but if I am to be in heaven with God for eternity then I have no choice but to do what my son and I have willingly chosen to do!"

He then responded, "Isn't it enough that they are going to tear down, burn up, rehab, all the Christian Churches worldwide plus destroy any and everything that has to do with Christianity. Why do you have to allow this to happen to you? Why, I ask, as I am totally in the dark on your belief."?

I then said, "Look. You have been a good friend. Now it's time you let go and let us do what we must do. Thanks for your friendship, but it's done!" At that we said our goodbyes.

I went back to take a short nap. Soon the kids were home. I asked my daughter and son to join me in the living room after they got comfortable and had a bite to eat. We all sat and I said to my daughter, "Both your brother and I, as you well know, took our Christianity very serious. We both signed a form saying we won't renounce our belief so on September 9, in nine days, we are both going to be shot by a firing squad unless we either renounce our belief or the government changes its heart, which I doubt since they put the full blame of the vanishings and worldwide problems squarely on Christianity! So my reason in calling you in here is to let you know I am going to the title company and the bank tomorrow to transfer all our assets into your name and you're going to have to go down as well in order to sign and get fingerprinted for this new law. Is all this alright with you?"

At that she began crying as we both did as well, but soon she simply said, "If that's what has to be then so be it. What time do you want me to meet you and where?"

Within a week all was transferred into her name and her being of legal age there was no difficulty in doing so. It got to be the 8th of September and we got a phone call asking if we had changed our minds and we both said no. At that they said a car would be here at 10 A.M. to pick us up for the last ride of our lives.

With that we hung the phone up and again asked each other. "Are you sure?"

10 A.M. got here sooner than expected. We had both dressed in our normal daywear. My daughter stood at the door as we walked out to the car. A hug, a kiss, a tear, but soon we were on our way to the local jail. We got marched in and were asked once again if we would sign a Renouncement Form and once again we said no. With that we were put in a cell. Soon phone calls were made to get the final ok. The doors were all closed on all sides. A hooded man walked in with a pistol in his hand. He asked again, "Are you sure?"

We both nodded 'yes' and with that he pulled up his gun and shot my son first right in the heart and next he shot and killed me!

This is his daughter now writing to let you know what happened afterwards. I was called to ask if I would like to make funeral arrangements. I said yes. Two days later we had my dad and brother's funeral and I had them buried next to mom. I also had an inscription put on both of their graves. "They believed in God to the death." After the funeral I went back to try to live a life without mom, dad and my best friend, my brother!

The beginning!

Chapter Eleven

BIBLICAL REFERENCES

Biblical References to This Story

SECOND CHANCE

1) Daniel 9:28	Old Testament
2) Matthew 24:35-44	New Testament
3) Mark 13:32-37	New Testament
4) 2nd Timothy 3:1-9	New Testament
5) Jude 1:14-16	New Testament

These are but a small portion of the words spoken
in the Holy Bible of Jesus Christ return.
It may happened today, tonight or a thousand years
from now, but you can take it to the bank,
God will bring it to pass, guaranteed!

DANIEL 7:9-28

I watched as thrones were put in place and the ancient of days-The Almighty God-sat down to judge. His clothing was as white as snow, his hair like whitest wool. He sat upon a fiery throne brought in on flaming wheels, and a river of fire lowed from before him. Millions of Angels ministered to Him and hundreds of millions of people stood before Him, waiting to be judged. Then the court began its session and the books were opened.

As I watched, the brutal fourth animal was killed and its body handed over to be burned because of its arrogance against Almighty God, and the boasting of its little horn. As for the other three animals, their kingdoms were taken from them, but they were allowed to live a short time longer.

Next I saw the arrival of a man, or so he seemed to be, brought there on clouds from heaven; he approached the ancient of days and was presented to him. He was given the ruling power and glory over all the nations of the world, so that all people of every language must obey Him. His power is eternal, it will never end; his government shall never fall.

I was so confused and disturbed by all I had seen, Daniel wrote in his report, so I approached one of those standing beside the throne and asked him the meaning of all these things, and he explained them to me.

"These four huge animals," he said "represent four kings who will someday rule the earth. But in the end the people of the most high God shall rule the governments of the world forever and forever."

Then I asked about the fourth animal, the one so brutal and

shocking, with its iron teeth and brass claws that tore men apart and that stamped others to death with its feet. I asked, too, about the ten horns and the little horn that came up afterward and destroyed three of the others, the horn with the eyes, and the loud, bragging mouth, the one which was stronger than the others. For I had seen this horn warring against God's people and winning, until the ancient of days came and opened his court and vindicated his people, giving them worldwide powers of government.

"This fourth animal," he told me, "is the fourth world power that will rule the earth. It will be more brutal than any of the others; it will devour the whole world, destroying everything before it. His ten horns are ten kings that will rise out of his empire; then another king will arise, more brutal than the other ten, and will destroy three of them. He will defy the most high God and wear down the saints with persecution and try to change all laws, morals, and customs. God's people will be helpless in his hands for three and a half years.

"But then the ancient of days will come and open his court of justice and take all power from this vicious king, to consume and destroy it until the end. Then every nation under heaven, and all their power, shall be given to the people of God; they shall rule all things forever, and all rulers shall serve and obey them."

That was the end of the dream. When I awoke, I was greatly disturbed, and my face was pale with fright, but I told no one what I had seen.

JUDE 1:14-16

Enoch, who lived seven generations after Adam, knew about these men and said this about them, "See the Lord is coming with millions of His Holy Ones. He will bring the people of the world before Him in Judgment to receive just punishment and to prove the terrible things they have done in rebellion against God, revealing all they had said against Him." These men are constant gripers, never satisfied, doing whatever evil they feel like; they are loudmouth "show-offs," and when they show respect for others, it is only to get something from them in return.

MATTHEW 24:35-44

Heaven and earth will disappear, but my words remain forever. But no one knows the date and hour when the end will be, not even the angels. No, nor even God's son. Only the Father knows.

"The world will be at ease – banquets and parties and weddings – just as it was in Noah's time before the sudden coming of the flood; people wouldn't believe what was going to happen until the flood actually arrived and took them all away. So shall my coming be.

"Two men will be working together in the fields, and one will be taken, the other left. Two women will be going about their household tasks; one will be taken, the other left.

"So be prepared, for you don't know what day your Lord is coming.

"Just as a man can prevent trouble from thieves by keeping watch for them, so you can avoid trouble by always being ready for my unannounced return."

MARK 24:35-37

"However, no one, not even the angels in heaven, nor I myself, knows the day or hour when these things will happen; only the Father knows. And since you don't know when it will happen, stay alert. Be on the watch (for my return).

"My coming can be compared with that of a man who went on a trip to another country. He laid out his employees' work for them to do while he was gone, and told the gatekeeper to watch for his return.

"Keep a sharp lookout! For you do not know when I will come, at evening, at midnight, early dawn or late daybreak. Don't let me find you sleeping. Watch for my return! This is my message to you and to everyone else."

2ND TIMOTHY 3:1-9

You may as well know this too. Timothy, that in the last days it is going to be very difficult to be a Christian. For people will love only themselves and their money. They will be proud and boastful, sneering at God, disobedient to their parents, ungrateful to them, and thoroughly bad. They will be hardheaded and never give in to others; they will be constant liars and troublemakers and will think nothing of immorality. They will be rough and cruel, and sneer at those who try to be good. They will betray their friends; they will be hotheaded, puffed up with pride, and prefer good times to worshipping God. They will go to church, yes, but they won't really believe anything they hear. Don't be taken in by people like that.

They are the kind who craftily sneak into other people's homes and make friendships with silly, sin-burdened women and teach them their new doctrines. Women of that kind are forever following new teachers but they never understand the truth. And these teachers fight truth just as Jannes and Jambres fought against Moses. They have dirty minds, warped and twisted, and have turned against the Christian faith.

But they won't get away with all this forever. Someday their deceit will be well known to everyone, as was the sin of Jannes and Jambres.

Printed in the United States
By Bookmasters